Roedd Nansi a Nel yn
chwilio am rywbeth.

Ond beth?

"Dim syniad eto," meddai'r ddwy,

"ond fe gawn ni hyd i rywbeth."

"Oooooooooooo."

"Aaaaaaaaa."

Tybed?

"Does wybod," meddai'r ddwy.

Does wybod beth?

"Wel ...

... !"

"Does wybod,"
meddai Nansi a Nel,

"nes rhoi cynnig arni!"

Rhoi cynnig ar beth?

"Popeth."

"Twît twît."

"Fflap fflap."

"Popeth sy'n werth chweil."

"Ti'n gweld?" meddai Nansi a Nel.

"Ffwrdd â ni."

LLITHRO

HEDFAN

DISGYN!

"Edrych!"

"Wy glas."

"Does wybod nes dod o hyd
iddo," meddai Nansi a Nel.

"A dyma ni wedi dod o hyd iddo!"

Mwy o straeon am Nansi a Nel:

Nansi a Nel a'r Wenynen Fach Brysur
Nansi a Nel a'r Diwrnod Glawog
Nansi a Nel a'r Cylch Tylwyth Teg
Nansi a Nel a'r Noson Olau Leuad
Nansi a Nel a'r Mwsog
Nansi a Nel a'r Gwenith Gwyn
Nansi a Nel a'r Awel Ysgafn
Nansi a Nel a'r Cwestiwn
Nansi a Nel a'r Ffordd Adref

This book is dedicated to the Lord!

"Shout for joy to the Lord, all the earth. Worship the Lord with gladness; come before him with joyful songs. Know that the Lord is God. It is he who made us, and we are his; we are his people, the sheep of his pasture. Enter his gates with thanksgiving and his courts with praise; give thanks to him and praise his name. For the Lord is good and his love endures forever; his faithfulness continues through all generations" (Psalm 100). Thank God for all of His provision to us and for making this book possible. Also, thanks be to God for my family who is so supportive! They are all a blessing to me every day from the Lord!

 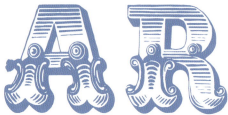

HE
AR
studio

art
cooking

cooking healthy recipes for both your hearts

He Art cooking
healthy recipes for both your hearts

Published by:
He Art studio
1008 East De La Guerra Street
Santa Barbara, CA 93103
www.nathanwoods.org
nw@nathanwoods.org

*Scripture quotations taken from the HOLY BIBLE,
NEW INTERNATIONAL VERSION. Copyright
© 1973, 1978, 1984 by International Bible
Society. Used by permission of Zondervan
Publishing House.*

Scriptures were sometimes located with the NIV
version of *Blue Letter Bible,* an online Bible
resource:
*THE HOLY BIBLE, NEW INTERNATIONAL
VERSION®, NIV® Copyright © 1973, 1978, 1984
by International Bible Society® Used by permission. All rights reserved worldwide.*

ISBN: 978-0-9854053-9-7

Printed in China by:
Wai Man Book Binding (China) Ltd.
Flat A, 9/F., Phase 1, Kwun Tong Industrial
Centre, 472-484 Kwun Tong Road, Kwun Tong,
Kowloon, Hong Kong S.A.R.
www.waiman-bookbinding.com
info@waiman-bookbinding.com
(852) 2793 5657

12 11 10 9 8 7 6 5 4 3 2 1

Praise the LORD for leading all production!

Design: Nathan Woods under God's direction

Scientific Research and Editing: Nick Woods under God's direction

Language Editors: Megan Staropoli for French; Michele Capizzi and Giovanni Goss, with *Piazza Italia,* for Italian, and Manuel Antoñio Hernandez Sanchez Jr. aka Chach for Spanish, all under God's direction

Executive Printing Managers: Nathan Woods with He Art, and David Lui with Wai Man Book Binding, under God's direction

Additional Printing Managers: Robert Jacobs, Connie Summey, Carla Galbraith, Sharon Sands, and David Klatt, all under God's direction

Special thanks to:

Piazza Italia
1129 NW Johnson Street
Portland, OR 97209
www.piazzaportland.com
(503) 478-0619

Door of Hope
Hinson Annex
1315 SE 20th Avenue
Portland, OR 97214
www.doorofhopepdx.org

Elephants Delicatessen
115 NW 22nd Avenue
Portland, OR 97210-3503
www.elephantsdeli.com
(503) 299-6304

All under God's direction! Everything is for Him and He is always there for us with love!

Jesus is the Way and the Truth and the Life

As you turn the pages of this book, the 'Table of Contents' can help you to find your way. In life, God is our guide and will help us find the Way, that being Jesus, His one and only Son. May we continue to seek Him in all we do, for He is Who we are looking for. He completes us. "Jesus answered, 'I am the way and the truth and the life. No one comes to the Father except through me" (John 14:6). His relationship gives us life. "'For in him we live and move and have our being.' As some of your own poets have said, 'We are his offspring'" (Acts 17:28). He is our God. "In that day they will say, 'Surely this is our God; we trusted in him, and he saved us. This is the LORD, we trusted in him; let us rejoice and be glad in his salvation'" (Isaiah 25:9). By reading the 'recipes' of Scripture from Him, I pray that we can realize He is always with us, waiting in love, for us to turn to Him and believe. "For this God is our God for ever and ever; he will be our guide even to the end" (Psalm 48:14). Hallelujah for Him being the Way, Truth and Life for us!

Table of Contents

Salty without Salt

Jesus said to His disciples, "You are the salt of the earth. But if the salt loses its saltiness, how can it be made salty again? It is no longer good for anything, except to be thrown out and trampled by men. You are the light of the world. A city on a hill cannot be hidden. Neither do people light a lamp and put it under a bowl. Instead they put it on its stand, and it gives light to everyone in the house. In the same way, let your light shine before men, that they may see your good deeds and praise your Father in heaven" (Matthew 5:13-16).

Jesus said, "You *are* the salt of the earth . . . You *are* the light of the world." For a long time I had read this as, "*Be* the salt of the earth . . . *Be* the light of the world." However, this is really quite impossible and frustrating without Jesus. Instead of relying on our own power, Jesus encourages us to live in Him (John 14:6)! Jesus' love and light naturally shines through His disciples, i.e., His followers! In this book, there are many recipes that include low sodium meals presented along with relevant Scripture. With both, you have the opportunity to be salty in the LORD, but won't have to make yourself physically unhealthy. Indeed, you don't have to eat a lot of salt to be *salty!*

After living with hypertension for a while, I realized that there is salt in almost everything. If you have to watch your salt intake, this should be the perfect book. If you don't have to, this book will be *salty* for you in the Way of Jesus. Enjoy the healthy recipes for both your hearts. God Bless and praise our Father in heaven for making this book and all things possible!

J'en voud-
rais sans
sel s'il vo-
us plaît

Bananas, Blueberries, Strawberries, Avocados, Melons, Kiwis, Mangos . . .

An Introduction to Sodium and Potassium

Why is too much sodium unhealthy for your heart?

After we eat a meal, the nutrients from the food are carried to our body's cells via the bloodstream. Our recommended daily intake of sodium - 2300 mg for most people and 1500 mg or less for those with high blood pressure - is often surpassed, and any excess dietary sodium accumulates in the bloodstream.[1] When there is a dissolved substance in the blood, water also enters to regulate the concentration of solutes. So, one reason that sodium elevates blood pressure is because it increases the volume of fluid within blood vessels. Though, there are many other and more complicated reasons that blood pressure rises in response to sodium.[2] Sugar too, in high amounts, has recently been discovered as a substance that increases blood pressure.[3] Sustained high blood pressure is unhealthy for your heart because your heart has to work harder against all the force! Let's help our bodies out (1 Corinthians 6:19-20)!

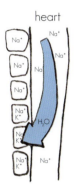

heart

How potassium lowers your blood pressure:

Again, the reasons behind this physiological process are complex, so here is one simplified explanation (see footnotes 1-3). Potassium ions (K$^+$) enter the cells of your body more passively than sodium ions (Na$^+$). Whenever potassium ions enter cells, it causes a reversal of the osmosis described above (there is now a higher concentration of solutes inside the cells than in the blood, so water leaves the blood and enters cells). By drinking more water, your body will flush out excess sodium and lower your blood pressure![4] Shown in the photo are a variety of fruits that are high in potassium. For a more complete list of potassium rich foods see pg. 220.

If you are worried about salt intake or anything, don't be! There are many things to do to lower your blood pressure or solve your problems. Jesus' help to us is always the best. He assures us, "Therefore I tell you, do not worry about your life, what you will eat or drink; or about your body, what you will wear. Is not life more important than food, and the body more important than clothes? Look at the birds of the air; they do not sow or reap or store away in barns, and yet your heavenly Father feeds them. Are you not much more valuable than they? Who of you by worrying can add a single hour to his life?" (Mark 6:25-27). Don't worry, because Jesus will provide you with just what you need in Him. All we have to do is ask (see Matthew 7:7; James 4:3; and 'Crab Cakes!,' pg. 96)!

An Introduction to Oils and Fats

Introduction

There are both healthy and unhealthy fats. Even in the Bible some fats are desired and some are undesired. When Abel offered his sacrifice to God, God was pleased with the fat because he sacrificed through faith. "But Abel brought fat portions from some of the firstborn of his flock. The LORD looked with favor on Abel and his offering" (Genesis 4:4; see also Hebrews 11:4).[63c] Jesus has now replaced these sacrifices because He died on the cross for our sins. This is why we are no longer like Cain, who had a sacrifice that was not acceptable. Jesus' work on the cross is a perfect sacrifice for all of us, resembling the fat that Abel offered to God. He was the final and best offering. Thank God! There are times, though, when fat is seen as undesirable. God speaks against those who deny Him. He says, "Like cages full of birds, their houses are full of deceit; they have become rich and powerful and have grown fat and sleek. Their evil deeds have no limit; they do not plead the case of the fatherless to win it, they do not defend the rights of the poor" (Jeremiah 5:27-28).

Chemically speaking, too, there are healthy and unhealthy fats. Unsaturated fats are liquid at room temperature and are *healthy* because they promote the formation of high density lipoproteins (HDLs) and decrease the formation of low density lipoproteins (LDLs). In effect, they reduce your cholesterol and maintain clean blood vessels. Saturated and trans fats are both solid at room temperature. In general, they increase your blood pressure and risk of atherosclerosis.[5] Let us cut out saturated and trans fats from our diets and boost our intake of healthy unsaturated fats. Also, we can have 'good fat' in Jesus by trusting in Him! Below is a table of foods containing oil fats and their relative amounts of omega fatty acids.[6] Omega-3 prevents heart disease, promotes brain function, eye health and general health. Omega-6, found mostly in meat, is very healthy as well, but is often over consumed in toxic levels. Aim for less than a 1/3 ratio (omega-3 to omega-6).[7]

Food	Omega-3 (grams per 100 g)	Omega-6 (grams per 100 g)
Flax	20.3	4.9
Pumpkin seeds	3.2	23.4
Salmon	3.2	0.7
Walnuts	3.0	30.6
Soy beans	1.2	8.6
Olive oil	0.6	7.9
Sunflower seeds	0	30.7

An Introduction to Pasta and Carbs

Introduction

What is pasta?

Pasta consists mainly of flour and water. Water is one of the best substances for your body, and on average should make up about 60% of your body's weight.[4] The main type of flour used in pasta is wheat flour. It contains mostly carbohydrates or 'saccharides,' which means sugar, as well as fiber, protein and iron. There are many different types of non-wheat flours too, such as almond, acorn, brown rice, chestnut, chickpea, tapioca and quinoa for the gluten-free diet.[8]

What are carbohydrates and why are they important to eat?

Carbohydrates have many functions in the body such as providing energy storage and DNA structure.[9] In pasta, carbohydrates mostly come in the forms of starch and fiber. Starches are long chains of the simple sugar glucose. The common sugars besides glucose are sucrose and fructose. Sucrose is actually composed of glucose and fructose and is found commonly in fruits. Natural fructose is found in many foods as well, but is now also synthetically produced from corn. Why is all of this important? In our bodies, glucose is the only form of the sugar molecule that can be metabolized directly into energy. Any other form has to first be converted into glucose by a metabolic pathway or it will be stored as a lipid, or fat. The by-products of the sugar-conversion process, aldehydes, are unhealthy. Aldehydes actually impair protein function and are difficult to break down themselves. This is why pastas, or foods high in natural sugars, are much healthier for you!

It is important to eat pasta for the glucose, but *also* because of the high amounts of fiber. Fiber slows down the metabolic processing of sugar. Thus, there is more time for the fructose to be converted to usable energy rather than fat. This means less aldehyde production, less adipose tissue, and a healthier heart![10] Other foods that naturally contain high amounts of fiber besides pastas are fruits, vegetables, oats, and grains including brown rice and quinoa. When drinking fruit juices, consider the type of sugars and the amount of fiber, often found in pulp.

When thinking of all of this information, Jesus Loves! It may seem hard now to digest all of these sugars, but Jesus is like the fiber and He makes it possible to be healthier. In studying the Word, even if it may seem like it takes a long time, the results are healthy. We will learn so much and have happier hearts, plus it's not that long of a process! In 1 Corinthians 8:1, Paul reminds that, ". . . knowledge puffs up, but love builds up." Don't get confused with things that are so overwhelming at first. Remember that Jesus and His love for us are what the Scriptures are all about. How sweet!

Chinese BBQ Pork
Pork tenderloin marinated in Chinese BBQ sauce, then roasted & served with hot mustard & dipping sauce.
$13.25 / pound

Teriyaki Salmon with Wasabi Sauce
Salmon, soy sauce, ginger, mustard and wasabi powder & mayonnaise, sesame seeds
$15.95/lb

Greek Metala Salad
...a, red onions, bell peppers, ... Kalamata olives, feta cheese, ... lemon juice, olive oil, garlic, ...il & pepper.

Ratatouille Squares
Eggplant, bell peppers, onions, zucchini, yellow squash, olive oil, fresh herbs & tomatoes
$7.95 / each

Elephants House Salad
Baby greens, carrots, corn, cucumber, tomatoes, & Elephants own Slow ... olive oil, champagne vinegar, cherry ..., herbs, spices, and salt)
$4.50/lb

Pear Shaped Risotto
Arborio rice, butter, onions, vegetable stock, & parmesan cheese, with marinara sauce (olive oil, tomatoes, carrots, fresh basil, fresh rosemary, and garlic)
$8.00/lb

～ Tipi di Pasta ～

01 Penne Rigate *(ridged quills/ feathers)*

02 Penne Lisce *(smooth quills/ feathers)*

03 Tortiglioni *(thick twists/ pies)*

04 Conchiglie *(shells)*

05 Farfalle *(butterflies)*

06 Orecchiette *(little ears)*

07 Macaroni *(elbows)*

08 Ditali *(thimbles)*

09 Ditalini *(little thimbles)*

10 Orzo *(barley)*

11 Couscous *(to pound)*

12 Stellini *(little stars)*

13 Ravioli *(pillows)*

14 Fusilli corti *(short springs)*

15 Cavatappi *(corkscrews)*

16 Rotelle *(little wheels)*

17 Tortellini *(little hats)*

18 Capellini *(angel hair)*

19 Spaghettini *(thin spaghetti)*

20 Spaghetti *(little strings)*

21 Spaghettoni *(thick spaghetti)*

22 Fusilli lunghi *(long fusilli)*

23 Linguine *(little tongues)*

24 Fettuccine *(little ribbons)*

~Mangiamo pasta!

~Mangiamo la Sua Parola!

Pasta Table

. . . And speaking of pasta, here is a nice table that shows and describes many kinds.[193] With all of the different shapes and sizes, I can't help thinking of how they resemble people! Each one has it's own speciality or purpose. In terms of pasta, the smaller or more squiggly ones are best for heartier and meatier sauces. These sauces are usually darker in color and are tomato- or vegetable-based. The tubular types compliment cheeses and soups well (especially the shell pastas), and thinner, elongated pastas are great for light sauces and seafood.

And speaking of people, each person has their own special purpose! If you think of the first people Jesus called to follow Him, His disciples, they were actually quite a diverse group. As recorded in Matthew, the first four were fishermen. "'Come, follow me,' Jesus said, 'and I will make you fishers of men.' At once they left their nets and followed him" (Matthew 4:19). These men followed Jesus with what they knew; they fished for men, telling many about His love and promises to them. Phillip, another disciple, was a fisherman too, but his *questions* to Jesus reveal to us that Jesus is closer than we think. For in Luke 11:9, Jesus explains, "So I say to you: Ask and it will be given to you; seek and you will find; knock and the door will be opened to you." All we have to do is ask Jesus, and He is already there (see also pg. 96)! Matthew, another disciple, was initially a tax collector and rejected by many because of his career. He was called by Jesus and followed Him, showing that Christ is not for people who think they are 'good,' but rather for those who need help. When Jesus was eating with 'sinners' and tax collectors one day, the Pharisees were ridiculing Him. "On hearing this, Jesus said to them, 'It is not the healthy who need a doctor, but the sick. I have not come to call the righteous, but sinners'" (Mark 2:17). Jesus shows that we should humble ourselves and not think that we can earn Him. It is only through Jesus, and His sacrifice on the cross, that we are enabled to be with Him, not by our own works. Finally, there is Thomas. He actually had to see and touch Jesus to believe in Him. Jesus gladly let him: ". . . see my hands. Reach out your hand and put it into my side. Stop doubting and believe.' Thomas said to him, 'My Lord and my God!' Then Jesus told him, 'Because you have seen me, you have believed; blessed are those who have not seen and yet have believed'" (John 20:27-29). Jesus wants us to believe in Him by faith! He is risen indeed and is there for us! Whatever traits God has given you, no matter your shape or size, you are a gift that God has made to share with others about Him. Plus, you are beautifully made in His image (Genesis 1:27)! Let us all stop doubting and believe, and then tell others!

What are proteins?

Proteins are the basic building blocks for the body's cellular activities. One example of a protein structure is the sodium-potassium pump, which controls the exchange of two K^+ for three Na^+ between the blood and cells. This chemical balance and result was explained more in the 'Introduction to Sodium and Potassium,' but the protein structure is actually responsible for forming the channel.[11] Aquaporins are the proteins that control the flow of water in this system.[12] There are many proteins that our body depends on, some are even yet to be discovered.

What are amino acids?

Amino acids are the building blocks for proteins. Proteins functions change based on the sequence and amount of amino acids. The variations are similar to music, where just eight whole notes can be played many different ways. There are 20 different kinds of amino acids, 12 of which are produced naturally by your body and the other eight of which need to be consumed.[13] This is why these eight amino acids are termed 'essential,' because they are really necessary. Imagine trying to play a song and not having all of the notes!

The essential amino acids are isoleucine, leucine, lysine, methionine, phenylalanine, tryptophan, threonine, and valine, all of which should be consumed regularly. Meats, eggs, fish and dairy products contain a lot of these amino acids; however, if you can't eat these foods, there are many alternatives. Quinoa and soy are 'complete' proteins because they have these essential amino acids.[14] Brown rice is not complete by itself, but is when paired with beans. For a great way to look at food nutrition, visit nutritiondata.self.com and type in the food name.[15]

Making sure that we have our complete nutrition reminds me of a verse in Ephesians. Paul writes, "Therefore put on the full armor of God, so that when the day of evil comes, you may be able to stand your ground, and after you have done everything, to stand. Stand firm then, with the belt of truth buckled around your waist, with the breastplate of righteousness in place, and with your feet fitted with the readiness that comes from the gospel of peace. In addition to all this, take up the shield of faith, with which you can extinguish all the flaming arrows of the evil one. Take the helmet of salvation and the sword of the Spirit, which is the word of God" (Ephesians 6: 13-17). Forming a complete spiritual protection is paramount. In Christ we are protected and have victory as seen on the cross! Jesus defeated death on the cross when He arose, so those who abide in Him also have victory over death and its sting. Hallelujah!

How to Speak Salty

"Let your conversation be always full of grace, seasoned with salt, so that you may know how to answer everyone" (Colossians 4:6). Even when you are ordering a plate without salt, your conversation can be salty. In writing this book, I was largely influenced by the cultural cuisines of Italy, France and Mexico. Here is how to order food and say a few phrases in these three languages. Thanks God for culture!

	Française	Italiano	Español
I would like some . . . please.	Je voudrais des . . . s'il vous plaît.	Vorrei qualche . . . per favore.	Me gustaría un poco de . . . por favor.
Fruit	Fruits	Frutta	Fruta
Vegetables	Légumes	Verdure	Verduras
Bread/ Cheese	Pain/ Fromage	Pane/ Formaggio	Pan/ Queso
Pasta	Pâte	Pasta	Pasta
Fish/ Meat	Poisson/ Viande	Pesce/ Carne	Pescado/ Carne
Beans	Haricots	Fagioli	Frijoles
Salad	Salade	Insalata	Ensalada
This one (m/ f)	Celui-ci/ Celle-ci	Questo/ Questa	Este/ Esta
To-go/ For here	A emporter/ Sur place	Da portare via/ Per qui	Para llevar/ Para aquí
I would like it without salt please.	J'en voudrais sans sel s'il vous plaît.	Non lo voglio con il sale, per favore.	Sin sal por favor.
Which one (m/ f) has the least salt?	Lequel/ Laquelle a le moins de sel?	Quale ha il minimo sale?	¿Cuál tiene la menor cantidad de sal?
A little . . . more/ less of	Un peu . . . plus/ moins de	Un po . . . 'più/ meno di	Un poco . . . más/ menos de
Thank you	Merci	Grazie	Gracias
You're welcome	De rien	Prego	De nada
God Bless!	Que Dieu vous bénisse!	Dio vi benedica!	Dios los bendiga!

Pan Care

When cooking it's effective to use nonstick surfaces. However, there are some important safety measures that should be employed to use these surfaces healthily. Nonstick surfaces are generally nonleaching under low temperatures, but can leach harmful compounds at high temperatures.[16] Be sure to always cook under the specific guidelines as suggested by your cookware manufacturer, and use nonabrasive spatulas.[17] I would recommend using wood because plastics and their components can leach.[18] Continual use of plastics in cooking over the years can be unhealthy.[19]

There are many alternatives to nonstick surfaces, and when used correctly are actually easy to cook with and clean. Cast iron and stainless steel are great options, not only because of their longevity in the kitchen, but also because of their even heat distribution.

Cast iron pans have many culinary uses and are often very affordable, especially if passed on from family. Additionally, they leach no harmful elements (if some iron does get into your food, it will help you, not harm you). In order to maintain a truly nonstick surface though, the pan must be 'seasoned' or 'cured,' otherwise you will end up with quite a mess. To season pans, simply rub all surfaces with a saturated fat, such as shortening or lard. Avoid using butter because of the extra ingredients that break down the pan and cause rust (washing with soap also causes rust). Place the pan in an oven or barbeque and set to 450°F - 500°F with aluminium foil below. After half an hour, let the pan cool and repeat as necessary. Upon each use, clean the pan without soap and rub more shortening or lard over the cooking surface. Following these steps will ensure many years of nonstick cooking. (Also, never use cold water on a hot cast iron pan or it might break.[20])

Stainless steel, and copper-lined stainless steel pans, are additional go-to items for a chef. The carbon in the steel will not hurt you when it comes off the pan, and the food's flavor remains true. Each use may cause the food to stick slightly, especially when cooking fish or with garlic, but it is easily cleaned afterwards. When finished cooking, pour a few cups of water into the already warm pan (make sure it is not hot). Turning to high heat, cover and let steam for about 3 minutes. When slightly cooled, wash with soap and water. The debris should come off very easily.

All of this talk of metal makes me think of the verse, "As iron sharpens iron, so one man sharpens another" (Proverbs 27:17). Learning more about how to become healthier, with cookware or anything, sharpens one another, but loving people in Jesus' Name is the best (Mark 12:30-31)! We are reminded in Romans 2:4, "... God's kindness leads you toward repentance ..." Jesus loves us!

Appetizers

Hors d'œuvres
Antipasti
Aperitivos

Bread of Life

Let's start with one of the most important meals. Right before Jesus was taken to be crucified, He was having dinner and sharing communion with His disciples. "While they were eating, Jesus took bread, gave thanks and broke it, and gave it to his disciples, saying, 'Take and eat; this is my body.' Then he took the cup, gave thanks and offered it to them, saying, 'Drink from it, all of you. This is my blood of the covenant, which is poured out for many for the forgiveness of sins. I tell you, I will not drink of this fruit of the vine from now on until that day when I drink it anew with you in my Father's kingdom.' When they had sung a hymn, they went out to the Mount of Olives" (Matthew 26:26-30). Jesus gave His own life for us. He did this to take our place for our sins. So even when we fall short and are wrong, He is there for us and can forgive us when we ask and trust in Him. Taking part in communion is important to do with friends and loved ones to remember the One who first loved us. "For God so loved the world that he gave his one and only Son, that whoever believes in him shall not perish but have eternal life. For God did not send his Son into the world to condemn the world, but to save the world through him" (John 3:16-17).

In John 6:35-37 Jesus also described how He is the bread of life. "Then Jesus declared, 'I am the bread of life. He who comes to me will never go hungry, and he who believes in me will never be thirsty. But as I told you, you have seen me and still you do not believe. All that the Father gives me will come to me, and whoever comes to me I will never drive away.'" Jesus, and His words to us, are just as important as physical food. Jesus even says that, "Man does not live on bread alone, but on every word that comes from the mouth of God" (Matthew 4:4). Jesus, the Word to us, as recorded in the Bible, is daily food! It is important to read and remember how Jesus loves and that He offers us forgiveness. When we take communion, let's recall what He did and why He did it. "A man ought to examine himself before he eats of the bread and drinks of the cup. For anyone who eats and drinks without recognizing the body of the Lord eats and drinks judgment on himself. That is why many among you are weak and sick, and a number of you have fallen asleep" (1 Corinthians 11:28-30).[2] Let's not forget though, Jesus loves us so much! This is a joyous occasion. After they took communion, Jesus and His close friends sang a hymn together. The mood of the occasion *then* may have been sad, but *now* Christ is alive and risen! Let us sing and celebrate Jesus' victory on the cross in joy by taking communion and remembering what He did for us.

Jesus taught His disciples how to pray. He said, "This, then, is how you should pray: "'Our Father in heaven, hollowed be your name, your kingdom come, your will be done on earth as it is in heaven. Give us today our daily bread. Forgive us our debts, as we also have forgiven our debtors. And lead us not into temptation, but deliver us from the evil one . . .† '"" (Matthew 6:9-13). We are taught that God would like us to come to Him, "And pray in the Spirit on all occasions with all kinds of prayers and requests" (Ephesians 6:18a), but following this prayer both verbatim and in structure is helpful to do so. Therefore, when we *talk* and *listen* to God (as we should always do), it is important to first recognize Him as God, and thank Him! He is God! Additionally, we should desire His will done and not our own, in order to bring His real goodness to earth. Then, Jesus teaches we should forgive others just as He forgave us, and ask not be led into temptation, actively praying against spiritual evil. And finally, we get to praise Him because everything is in His hands! Knowing these structural elements when we pray helps God's love and peace reign. So, let's pray to Him, "with all kinds of prayers and requests," but always keep the LORD's prayer in mind and heart.

There are several methods by which we can have our daily bread provided by God including: His Word as recorded in the Bible, because Jesus is the, "bread of life" (John 1:1-3, 14; 6:35; the main loaf); His daily provision, like manna (Exodus 16:32); and His constant insights into Him, through the Holy Spirit, as we seek Him (Matthew 7:7). Thank you God!

Just like there are several types of daily spiritual bread, there are several ways to make bread! This one here I first discovered in France. Initially, it may seem a bit odd, but it's delicious. The effect is similar to pan frying bread with olive oil. To make this surprising treat, simply place cheese, garlic, and any other desired topping in between slices of your favorite *miche de pain*. Drizzle with olive oil, and wrap with tin foil. Cook on the barbeque or stove top for 5-7 minutes. Remember that we can put bread into our stomachs for physical health, but it is far more important to put daily *bread* into our hearts for Him.

†Or *from evil; some late manuscripts one, / for yours is the kingdom and the power and the glory forever. Amen.*

Preheat oven or grill to at least 300°F (*consider making along with grilled meat or vegetables*)

1 loaf of bread

Pepper jack cheese (*try mozzarella or ricotta for fun variations*)

4 garlic cloves, minced

Extra virgin olive oil

1 sheet of tin foil

BBQ'ed Vegetables

Vegetables are sometimes overlooked. However, they have many great nutrients including fiber, vitamins and minerals. Eating them daily is important. Though, it can be tedious to eat them the same way every day. Below is a process to barbeque them straight on the grill. Other methods include pan frying, steaming, wrapping whole vegetables in foil to bake or barbeque them in their skins, and blanching (from the French verb *blanchir*, meaning *to whiten*). This last process involves boiling the vegetables in water until crisp and then immediately throwing them into an ice bath to stop the cooking process (in Italian, these vegetables could be referred to as *al dente* or *to the teeth*, a term usually used for pastas, but generally referring to a crisp texture [22]).

It's also fun and healthy to cook with different kinds of vegetables. Try some new squash or a beet in a style that you haven't before and see where you're led in His Spirit. Being adventurous and trying new approaches is how we grow in cooking and in life. When reading the Bible too, try different passages that you haven't read before or read a different *amount* than before. Some days a Gospel message might be a great place for a few minutes, and another day, reading a large part of the Old Testament would be fun. The stories and lessons in the Bible are so nutritious. And, like vegetables, they may seem boring at first, but when approached with a positive attitude, give lots of lessons and a healthy heart. I usually find that I read out of the New Testament, so I have been looking into the Old Testament recently. One passage that really stuck out to me was Daniel 6. This is when Daniel was in the Lion's den. At the end the king says of God, "For he is the living God and he endures forever; . . ." (6:26b). I would encourage you to read the passage and pray to God thanking Him for all the ways He has helped you!

To make the grilled vegetables, first select your produce. Try a variety of choices in color and texture. To prepare the grill, preheat to at least 400°F. While the grill is warming, place your produce on skewers in bite sized portions and marinate in a pan with extra virgin olive oil, garlic and herbs. Be careful when using metal skewers, because they may look cool but can get very hot. Cook and rotate with tongs for about 10 minutes or until there is slight charring on all sides. Serve warm with any main course and enjoy the variety not only in vegetables, but in learning about God!

Red Gold and Yukon Gold small potatoes

Cherry tomato varieties [23]

Bell pepper varieties

Red or yellow onions

Zucchini

Broccoli

Olive oil, garlic and herbs

Jesus teaches us not to worry, but instead to trust in Him and in His promise of love. In Luke there is a beautiful illustration of how not to worry in an everyday life situation. It reads, "As Jesus and his disciples were on their way, he came to a village where a woman named Martha opened her home to him. She had a sister called Mary, who sat at the Lord's feet listening to what he said. But Martha was distracted by all the preparations that had to be made. She came to him and asked, 'Lord, don't you care that my sister has left me to do the work by myself? Tell her to help me!' 'Martha, Martha,' the Lord answered, 'you are worried and upset about many things, but only one thing is needed. Mary has chosen what is better and it will not be taken away from her'" (Luke 10:38-42). Jesus' words are perfect. When we come to Him and listen, we can realize that He has everything under control, and because of Him we are enabled to help others. Additionally, He teaches that preparing for guests is not about the type of food, or the cleanliness of the house, but rather that people are listening to the LORD.

In this preparation, I didn't have much but leftovers. No worries though! I quickly took a picture of the small amount of chicken, bread, mozzarella, basil and tomato. This amount was enough for the nice conversation that followed with my lifelong friend Jordan Johnson. When entertaining guests, even if you can't supply them with food, make sure you are first listening to Jesus. Then, if it is the LORD's will, take what you have and be creative with it. This is enough. The people you have over will feel much more welcomed if you can supply them with the LORD's love rather than luxuries. So listen to Him and everything else will follow.

First, listen to Jesus! To make a plate of leftovers afterwards, use a similar strategy as when making a vegetable spread. Aim for variation in color and texture. The process of laying them out should make many interesting and surprising combinations. My friend, Ben Ingalls, termed this process, 'plating.' He describes, "For me the concept of plating is about making food fun. Cooking is where there is a lot of creativity and work and effort. But plating is where you get people to really say 'wow.'"[24] Truly, if you spend time in God's Word and approach Him with thanks, it will be much easier to hear what He is putting on your plate each new day!

1 lb chicken or protein (see pg. 17). Sear chicken on high heat, reduce to low, cover, then let steam until flaky not rubbery.

Buffalo mozzarella, fresh basil from the garden, 1 tomato, and French bread (try salt free: pg. 219)

1/4 lemon

The spices that you have!

Humus, hummus, houmous, or hummous are all derived from the same Turkish spelling of the word *humus*.[25] The root, humus, itself means *mashed chick peas*, but in English commonly refers to *earth or soil*.[26] Many English transliterations work, but here the use of the spelling, 'Humus,' helps to impart a great lesson. The word *humble* actually means *lowly*, or *from the ground*, both of which also denote humus.[26] And Jesus teaches us that we must be humble. In fact, it is recorded in Genesis that, "The LORD God formed the man from the dust of the ground and breathed into his nostrils the breath of life, and the man became a living being" (Genesis 2:7). God created and made us from nothing into something, all by His power. He wants us to know that we exist because of Him. Thus, without Him, we are still like dirt, but in Christ and through His Holy Spirit, we have His life. This is why many verses say things like, "The LORD sustains the humble but casts the wicked to the ground" (Psalm 147:6). God is really just putting them back in their place so that they remember where they came from. He is rejecting their false pride and actually helping them so that they realize they could not exist without Him.

God loves those who are humble because then it is His working in them and His love in them that everyone can enjoy. When we work on our own, and pridefully think that we don't need Him, everyone misses out on His relationship. Jesus says, "Come to me, all you who are weary and burdened, and I will give you rest. Take my yoke upon you and learn from me, for I am gentle and humble in heart, and you will find rest for your souls" (Matthew 11:28-29). God's plan is that we can rest in Him and enjoy Him. This was made possible by Jesus, God's Son, who was truly humble, taking our place on the cross to present Himself to God on our behalf.

1/2 lb raw chickpeas (*garbanzo beans*) soaked overnight

1 lemon and lime to taste

1 (*+1/2 for garnish*) Tbsp olive oil

2 (*+1/2 for garnish*) Tbsp cilantro

Dried cumin, chili powder, pine nuts and paprika for garnish (*optional*)

Humus is a delightful treat, but is often loaded with sodium in the stores. Thankfully, making it at home is quick and entertaining. Start at least a day in advance to allow the chickpeas to soak in water overnight (use twice the amount of water). The next day, combine the chick peas, lemons, limes, 1 Tbsp of olive oil, 2 Tbsp of cilantro and spices into a blender or food processor. When the humus is thick enough for your liking, dip with some pita bread and recall humus in the LORD as well!

Bruschetta al Pomodoro

Bruschetta (pronounced 'brru-s'kay-tah') is a delicious and simple treat to make. This Italian appetizer derives its name from the verb *bruscare* which means *to roast over coals*. The title really refers to just the toasted bread rubbed with garlic and olive oil, however, it is commonly mistaken as the entire dish. There are several toppings besides the chopped tomatoes, including ham, garlic creams, and tapenads (olive-based spreads).[27] I also recall learning in Italy that bruschetta came about as a method to save bread that was going stale. Thank God for resourcefulness!

Bruschetta is one of my favorite appetizers to make, not only because of the tangy tomato and garlic bite, but because it was one of the first meals I made. It was a pleasant afternoon in Italy and my friend, Geoff Jensen, invited the idea. After getting the amounts of olive oil and basil just right, we had a pleasant meal together. At this inaugural meal, I learned that recipes and individual amounts of ingredients are relative to your taste. From then on, cooking has become more of an artistic expression, rather than a rote following of recipes. This idea that God planted in me has now culminated in this cookbook, and reminds me of the verses in Philippians 1:5-6. Paul writes to the Philippian Church and tells them that, "Because of your partnership in the gospel from the first day until now, being confident of this, that he who began a good work in you will carry it on to completion until the day of Christ Jesus." Before Jesus went to heaven, He promised all of us that He would send the Holy Spirit. The Holy Spirit guides us and carries out God's work in our lives when we abide in Him. I'm convinced that this cookbook would not have been possible without His guidance, and I'm assured every day He is available to help me or anyone who abides in Him. "Trust in the LORD with all your heart and lean not on your own understanding; in all your ways acknowledge him, and he will make your paths straight" (Proverbs 3:5-6).

To make this bruschetta's topping, first mix the ingredients proportionately in a bowl and adjust to taste. Use about 1 Tbsp of olive oil and go light on the strong balsamic vinegar. For the bruschetta itself, reserve some garlic, at least 3-4 cloves, and rub onto pieces of sliced bread placed on a cooking sheet. Drizzle some olive oil over all surfaces (I also add Parmesan cheese here) and broil at 500°F for 2-4 minutes, watching it well. When still hot, spread the tomatoes and enjoy the art of cooking and trusting in Him!

1 loaf of bread

7 Roma or Heirloom tomatoes

1 1/3 cups red onions

2/3 cup chopped basil

10 garlic cloves (*3-4 for bread*)

Olive oil, lemon, balsamic vinegar, and Parmesan to taste

Broccolini e Asparagi

Broccolini (or *little broccoli*) and asparagus go very well together. The subtle herbaceous flavor and the delicate crunch exist uniquely and yet similarly in each food. This combination reminds me of two very similar proverbs. The first is Proverbs 15:17, which says, "Better a meal of vegetables where there is love than a fattened calf with hatred." The preceding verse says, "Better a little with the fear of the LORD than great wealth with turmoil" (Proverbs 15:16). Jesus tells us to love one another and to love Him first. When we are focused instead on wealth, our possessions, or the food we eat, then God isn't the focus, and we loose sight of Love (1 John 4:8). All of us can relate to these verses on some level, and should remember that when we start heading in our own directions, we are moving away from the One who first made us and loved us.

One story that stands out explaining the meaning of a fattened calf is the parable of the prodigal son in Luke 15:20-24. At the end, the son realizes how he had sinned against heaven and the father, "So he got up and went to his father. 'But while he was still a long way off, his father saw him and was filled with compassion for him; he ran to his son, threw his arms around him and kissed him. 'The son said to him, 'Father, I have sinned against heaven and against you. I am no longer worthy to be called your son.' 'But the father said to his servants, 'Quick! Bring the best robe and put it on him. Put a ring on his finger and sandals on his feet. Bring the fattened calf and kill it. Let's have a feast and celebrate. For this son of mine was dead and is alive again; he was lost and is found.' So they began to celebrate." The son realized his mistake and went back to the father, confessing his sins. The father gladly gave him his best right away and everyone celebrated.

Sometimes in life we will have a meal of vegetables, and other times, more fancy meals. In every situation, remember it is most important to love God first and to love your neighbor as yourself (Mark 12:28-31). To make these vegetables, start by heating a pan to at least 400°F. Throw in the vegetables, and any spices, with your desired amount of olive oil (you may also try steaming, by placing the vegetables on a metal rack above boiling water). Add the almonds and garlic at the end as these tend to burn easily. When there is slight charring, serve immediately. Remember to love, and *how* God offers His love and His best gifts to all of us with His Son (John 14:6)!

About 10 broccolini stalks

About 15 asparagus stems

1/3 orange bell pepper

Extra virgin olive oil

2 Tbsp slivered almonds

4 chopped garlic cloves

Fresh black pepper to taste

Salads

Salades
Insalate
Ensaladas

Creative Salad

Let's get creative and praise the LORD! God has given us so many prime ingredients. The creative salad is a process to find new combinations with them and get your thinking cap on for Him. Started by my friend Ben Ingalls and I, this salad had always been a fun experimental project. We would enjoy a unique combination such as: avocados (a very necessary ingredient), strawberries, apples, lots of red onions, bell peppers and greens. We would often add dry-roasted, unsalted sunflower seeds, or slivered almonds for variation, and use olive oil and citrus for dressings. Nowadays, this salad has grown in appreciation within my own family. My mom really likes fetta cheese, so that usually finds it's way as a garnish (the potassium in the avocados helps to cancel out the sodium in the cheese, but always watch cheese intake with low-sodium diets). For your next salad or meal, whatever the ingredients, get creative and approach it as an opportunity to use inventiveness for Him. God loves it when we do and share with others, because His creativity is magnified!

"Enter his gates with thanksgiving and his courts with praise; give thanks to him and praise his name" (Psalm 100:4). The reason that this salad, cookbook, food, or anything should exist is to praise the LORD! For it is said, "Let everything that has breath praise the LORD. Praise the LORD" (Psalm 150:6). Psalm 100's cantation begins by entering His gates with thanksgiving, and the last Psalm in the book of Psalms ends with thanksgiving as well. This tells us that praising and thanking God is important. That is why the dedication page (the first page of this book) and the last page thank God, for nothing is possible without Him![128] Thanking God for just existing, for making such fine ingredients, or for anything, though, is not to flatter Him. Rather, by worshiping God, we come to know Him more and realize how good He is! It helps us follow Him and realize the joy that He freely gives.[129] And thanking God and worshiping Him can be done in other ways besides singing. It is a very common way, but Romans 12:1-8 speaks about how anything God gives us can be used for Him. Paul, the writer of Romans, elaborates in verses 6-8, "We have different gifts according to the grace given to us. If a man's gift is prophesying, let him use it in proportion to his faith. If it is serving, let him serve; if it is teaching, let him teach; if it is contributing to the needs of others, let him give generously; if it is leadership, let him govern diligently, if it is showing mercy, let him do it cheerfully." God openly offers grace to us all through His Son Jesus Christ, who paid the price for our sins. Thank God for His kindness in whatever gifts He has given you, believe in His work, and remember to metaphorically, "Sing to him a new song; play skillfully, and shout for joy" (Psalm 33:3).

Insalate

Caprese salad is a truly elegant meal. There are only three main ingredients, yet such complex flavor. It takes you to Italy every time. I reference *elegant* in the mathematical sense; when something complicated is reduced to a simple formula (as with Albert Einstein's mass-energy equivalence, $E = mc^2$, part of his 'Theory of Relativity'). Following Einstein's train of thought, or understanding the beautiful relationships between these three salad ingredients, is too hard for me. One thing I do know though, is that if you remove one part of the recipe or the equation, the rest is incomplete. Tomato and basil just don't do the trick. Understanding and maintaining these relationships is similar to the Trinity. *Jesus* is God's only begotten Son, fully human and also fully God. Additionally, Jesus ascended to the *Father* in heaven after He rose from the dead, defeating sin and death on the cross! And, He promised us all His *Holy Spirit* (John 14:25-31) to guide and teach us in His physical absence. All three ingredients are there, working together as One. The Trinity is very complex, yet at the same time, should be enjoyed just like this salad, or Einstein's equation. Coming to full understanding may not be reached, but I am thankful that God is bigger than I can imagine. It is important to maintain all three parts of the Trinity, because without one part, God is not fully recognized.

The three parts of this salad and the three parts of the equation are not fully operable without *definitions* of the relationships. The metaphor may be extended, in that just as the olive oil, balsamic vinegar and pepper make a caprese salad complete, or the squared function makes Einstein's equation work, God is a God who operates through the bind of love (Colossians 3:14). 1 John 4:8 says, "Whoever does not love does not know God, because God is love." I may not be able to understand the Trinity in whole, but as a result of having it made freely available to me through the Gospel of Jesus Christ, I can definitely come to terms with it. God is beyond us, truly loves us, and is all about welcoming us into a relationship with Him. That is, a Holy Trinity relationship defined by love!

Making the caprese ('ka-prray-zay') is easy. Start by selecting your tomatoes, mozzarella (I would recommend mozzarella di bufala), and fresh basil. Cutting the tomatoes with a bread knife helps to avoid squishing. Set out your desired amounts of ingredients, drizzle generously with olive oil and balsamic vinegar, and add freshly ground black pepper to taste. Enjoy the complexity of the simplicity in God.

Roma (*plum*) tomatoes or Heirloom tomatoes

Buffalo mozzarella

Fresh basil

Extra virgin olive oil

Balsamic vinegar and freshly ground black pepper to taste

Sabrina's Quinoa Salad

Now this is a healthy meal! Made by Sabrina Walters, this salad is better termed a 'meal' because it is loaded with a full spectrum of nutrients. Based in quinoa, it is a complete protein food (as discussed in 'An Introduction to Proteins and Amino Acids'), and is also high in fiber (the benefits of fiber are presented in 'An Introduction to Pasta and Carbs'). Additionally, her salad contains many vegetables, can easily be made gluten-free, dairy-free, soy-free, vegan or vegetarian, and has almost no sodium! It can be prepared for any of your friends with ease.

2 cups quinoa

4 cups vegetable/ chicken broth

2 cans of rinsed black beans or 1 cup of raw black beans soaked overnight (less sodium)[t30]

2 avocados

About 1 cup of fresh vegetables[t31]

2 sweet peppers (a variety of colors is best)

1 sweet onion or a bunch of green onions

1 bunch of cilantro

2 limes

Cumin, ginger, chili powder, red pepper flakes and black pepper to taste

Sabrina is the mom of one of my closest friends, Thomas Walters. The Walters regularly host 'Family Dinners' on Thursday nights. During these fine gatherings, they each invite 2-3 guests who share in food and fellowship. I have always enjoyed going not only for the salad, but more so because of the warm environment. Jesus has made this possible. He is the source of true friendship. If you don't have close friends now, first look to Jesus for companionship. After that, seek out those who love Jesus, because then you'll find Him in those friendships, and His love is what we are all looking for. Jesus Himself said of friends, "Greater love has no one than this, that he lay down his life for his friends" (John 15:13). Jesus is the best example of this verse because He laid down His life for all of us, so that we can stand clean before God. Jesus was the sacrifice for our sins so that when we fall short, He takes the blame. This sounds like a good friend to me. Likewise, Jesus mentions how we can be good friends to Him. He says to His disciples, or followers, "You are my friends if you do what I command . . . This is my command: Love each other" (John 15:14, 17). Let's join in the friendship, loving Him who first loved us (1 John 4:19) and all others!

To make the salad, start at least a day in advance. Begin by making a broth and soaking the beans in twice the amount of water overnight (steps for making a broth are in footnote 40). The next day, rinse the quinoa and put in a large pot (or rice maker) with twice the amount of strained broth. Cover and let simmer for 10-15 minutes. Add all other ingredients to your taste. It's really that simple, and His friendship is too!

Salmon Salad

I can almost taste the natural sesame seed flavor of the salmon married with the light olive oil and greens. My family and I made this salad one pleasant summer evening with our dear friend Barbara Setnicker. There is so much to say about Barbara, including how she is a grandmother figure in our family, and that she makes the best pies (see 'Rhubarbara Pie' on pg. 124), but I'll leave it to this here: The table setting was "so Barbara." My mother and I agreed that the blue place mats, the pink roses and the dishes reminded us of her (for a better view of the table spread, look at the chapter's Introduction). Identifying a person based on visual cues is such a common, and yet interesting phenomenon. Even back in the Old Testament age, people would identify other Christians by drawing an arc in the sand. If the other person was a Christian, they would finish the arc and make it into a fish.[32] Also, creation reveals to us a Creator. Paul records in Romans, "For since the creation of the world God's invisible qualities - his eternal power and divine nature - have been clearly seen, being understood from what has been made, so that men are without excuse" (Romans 1:20). Jesus and creation have already revealed God to us. Let us respond to God just as Christians responded to each other. And remember what Jesus said of demanding signs: "A wicked and adulterous generation asks for a miraculous sign! But none will be given it except the sign of the prophet Jonah. For as Jonah was three days and three nights in the belly of a huge fish, so the Son of Man will be three days and three nights in the heart of the earth" (Matthew 12:39-40). Jesus has risen from the dead and already revealed God to us. Asking for more signs shows we don't trust in the work God has done. Let's trust in Him with faith!

There are several ways to make the salmon. This sockeye recipe makes it sweet and charred, but for an alternate bleu cheese steamed method, please refer to pg. 89 (for salmon selection, see footnote 33). Start by removing the bones using a reserved set of tweezers and place the fillets into an olive oil laden pan. Set to high heat and add garlic, about 1/2 lemon, spices and olive oil. Sear for 5 minutes and toss the salad in the meantime. Reduce to a medium-low heat until the healthy fat rises to the top and flaking occurs. Now that it's ready, gently fold into the tossed salad, serve and respond to His handiwork with trust. Amen!

1 lb fresh salmon seasoned with 5 cloves of garlic, lemon and spices

4 oz mixed greens

3 oz unsalted sunflower seeds

3 green onions and 4 Tbsp of red onion

1 large Hass avocado

Olive oil, feta cheese, red pepper, and black pepper to taste (*try dill too*)

Salade aux Crevettes et Herbes

Crevettes, gamberetti, camarones, or *shrimps,* are tops in my book. I love shrimp! They have high amounts of protein per calorie, are low in saturated fat, and offer a fine source of Iron, Zinc, Vitamin D, B12, and B3. Additionally, they contain lots of omega-3 fatty acids which can reduce the risk of developing certain types of cancer.[34] All this said, they are really enjoyable to eat too, and if I have the occasion, I always go for shrimp.

A preference for seafood is one thing. Imagine though, if you could enjoy something nice all the time and have no harmful side effects, or never get bored (as our senses often get used to the same stimuli). In fact, *Jesus and His offer to us is the best thing available, and will leave us filled and at peace forever!* Jesus assures, "Whoever believes in me, as the Scripture has said, streams of living water will flow from within him" (John 7:38). Jesus said this to people who had a scarcity of water, the most important resource to them. And the peace and love that His Holy Spirit imparts is an unlimited source. Jesus offers His best to us, as seen when He laid down His life on the cross, and in how He offers "streams of living water" to all that simply believe for Him! Nothing that we can imagine even compares with how great it is to be united with God here and in heaven! Plus, just think, if God is all powerful, all knowing, and all loving, we will never reach the end of His *goodness* and can always enjoy the process of discovering how amazing He is. We will never grow tired and weary in heaven with God: "Never again will they hunger; never again will they thirst. The sun will not beat upon them, nor any scorching heat. For the Lamb at the center of the throne will be their shepherd; he will lead them to springs of living water. And God will wipe away every tear from their eyes" (Revelation 87:16-17). Jesus is offering us a huge promise and He already paid the price for it! All we have to do is respond and trust in Him with faith.

To make the salad, start by selecting fresh, large, uncooked shrimp (which are still grey-blue), because frozen varieties often contain lots of sodium or other preservatives. Devein and de-shell, then throw into a large, well olive-oiled pan. Set to high heat and add 1/2 lemon, red pepper flakes, chili powder, marjoram, and rosemary. Cook for about 5 minutes or until light-pink and flaky. Add garlic, serve with the tossed salad, and have faith in Him!

1/2 lb wild caught shrimp (*about 12 large shrimps*) with olive oil, 3-4 garlic cloves and spices

3 oz mixed greens

Ricotta shaved cheese or Parmesan shaved cheese

Microgreens to taste (*baby rose radish and baby broccoli*)

Rosemary, thyme, black pepper and extra virgin olive oil to taste

Insalata Italiana

This insalata Italiana has a warm place in my heart. It always reminds me of a favorite Italian restaurant that my family and I went to when we were younger. We would get salads similar to this one, follow them with minestrone soup, and finish by sharing a traditional square pizza. Even as a child, the healthiness of the food resonated with me at a certain level, but now that I'm older, I can appreciate how it was healthy. (Also, this salad would always come with a side of olive oil. I have grown used to using olive oil with citrus as a dressing and find it makes a great healthy choice.)

One place in Scripture that talks about the importance of food as a metaphor for God's Truth is Hebrews 5:12. It says, "In fact, though by this time you ought to be teachers, you need someone to teach you the elementary truths of God's Word all over again. You need milk, not solid food! Anyone who lives on milk, being still an infant, is not acquainted with the teaching about righteousness. But solid food is for the mature, who by constant use have trained themselves to distinguish good from evil." Seeking God's Truth, as revealed in Scripture, is like eating a full meal. If we are satisfied with just a small salad and milk, this nutrition would be a start. And Jesus' simple Truth is more than enough![†35] However, there is so much more to Him! He is very cool. Consider how as we grow older, we grow in our need of nutrition, so we add sprouts, legumes, peppers or proteins to our salads. Along with the variation, we realize and appreciate the amazingly gourmet and mature tastes. Let's treat God's Word the same way! *All of it* contains so much nutrition and flavor, so we should spend time with new Scriptures as well as old (Matthew 12:52; 2 Timothy 3:16)!

About 7 oz mixed spring greens

2 large vine tomatoes, quartered

1/2 red onion, sliced into crescents

Fresh cow or chevre mozzarella (*try thinly slicing or grading*)

Freshly ground black pepper

Recommended: pepperoncinis

Extra virgin olive oil on the side or to taste

I have always loved this salad and try to make it often. (To make this salad, simply combine all the ingredients!) Interestingly, this approach is similar to how I read the Bible. I actually read the Psalms, Proverbs, parts of the New Testament, and the Gospels quite often. This year though, I'm going to try to read more out of the Old Testament to learn from His amazing love in His-story. I encourage all of us to eat mature food, and learn about God's amazing love and depth, together (Ephesians 3:16-21)! Let us remember that He loves us and He gave His Only Son for us, so we don't need to earn His favor. But let us also remember to *grow* in His love by spending time with Him.

Couscous with Shrimp

This Mediterranean pasta salad is best served either hot or cold. I would not recommend serving it lukewarm though. Really, anything lukewarm is not that great either, being that it is at the perfect temperature to harvest bacteria. Interestingly, lukewarm is *room temperature*, and if you leave food to sit out it will *naturally* spoil. Why do I mention all of this? Jesus has a very similar teaching. He says, "So because you are lukewarm - neither hot nor cold - I am about to spit you out of my mouth" (Revelation 3:16). Jesus mentioned this to the Church in Laodicea whose members were not fully obeying Him. They were just going through the motions and didn't commit their hearts. God loves us so much that He gave His Only begotten Son, so when we refuse to join Him full-heartedly, it is insulting to Him and His great offer. The unrequited relationship can be seen as a husband (God) loving his wife (the Church), without the wife reciprocating His love (Ephesians 5:23)! That is crazy. God has complete mercy, but He is serious with what He says to lukewarm people. He desires a true relationship and offers it to us through *His Son's sacrifice* so that we can be with Him without sin separating us. And we all desire His Holy relationship. When we come to God, let's not be suscepti-ble to whatever the world is saying, or the environment around us, because it is often at a tempera-ture that easily harvests bacteria (and often we go unaware of our own putrification). Let's truly be available to God, for He has truly made Himself available to us in Love (1 John 3:16), and will always be there for us when we return to Him (Malachi 3:7).

To start this Mediterranean pasta salad, put the couscous in a large pot (or rice maker) with twice the amount of water. Also add the carrots, cilantro, and about 1/2 lime (plus some lemon if desired) with cumin and chili powder to taste. Cover and let simmer for 10-15 minutes. Meanwhile, start the shrimp. Devein and de-shell, then place into a well olive-oiled pan. Set to high heat, adding some more of the lime, lemon, and spices. (I would go light on the chili powder due to it's strength, but a little bit always accentuates the flavor of shrimp.) When the shrimp is light-pink and flaky, not rubbery, then it's finished. Combine the ingredients, using the remaining citrus, garlic and garnish, and remember to not be lukewarm! He loves you! (John 6:37)

1/2 lb couscous with 1/3 cup carrots, cilantro, lime and spices

1 lb wild caught shrimp (*about 24 large shrimps*) with olive oil, lime, 5-7 garlic cloves and spices

1/3 cup each of de-shelled sugar snap peas (*or unsalted frozen peas*), raisins, red onion and sweet onion

About 1/2 cup fresh cilantro

About 1/2 lemon and 1 1/2 limes, with cumin, chili powder, marjoram, black pepper and olive oil to taste

Soups

Soupes
Minestre
Sopas

Soups

Split pea soup is a perfect meal on a warm or cool day. The peas come in yellow and green varieties and offer tons of proteins, carbohydrates, fats and fiber. (Actually, split peas are one of the most fiber-dense foods, with 65% of your daily fiber in a 1 cup serving.[36] To learn more on the importance of fiber or the other components of nutrition, read pg. 12 and the 'Introduction' section.) You'll find that split peas make a light and nutritious meal, and when prepared with no sodium, leave you well fed and refreshed for the next activity.

This well fed and refreshed feeling is very similar to how you should feel being with the Holy Spirit, God's Spirit in you. He will take your burdens and give you hope. Jesus said, "Come to me all you who are weary and burdened, and I will give you rest. Take my yoke upon you and learn from me, for I am gentle and humble in heart, and you will find rest for your souls" (Matthew 11:28-29). God has promised that Jesus takes our sins upon Him. And speaking of split peas, God has 'split' our sins from us, for, "as far as the east is from the west, so far has he removed our transgressions from us" (Psalm 103:12). Jesus, the Psalms and everything in creation really, speak to how God offers forgiveness to us and loves us. God offered His Son for *all*, and is able to forgive any sin; nothing is too great for God's love! Your sins are forgiven when you are in Christ, because He took your place (Romans 8:1-2)! This is God's work, and not ours. *It's finished*, just as it was recorded, "When he received the drink, Jesus said, 'It is finished.' With that, he bowed his head and gave up his spirit" (John 19:30). Jesus has offered to save you, once and for all! Love Him back and receive His free gift! Also, you can share His love with others, even by offering them food in His Name.[37] Many are hungry so see what you can do to spread His love and be His hands and feet. God asks, "Is this not the kind of fasting I have chosen; to loose the chains of injustice and untie the cords of the yoke, to set the oppressed free and break every yoke? Is it not to share your food with the hungry and to provide the poor wanderer with shelter" (Isaiah 58:6-7a).

This meal is easy to prepare. Start a day in advance to allow the split peas to soak overnight in twice the amount of water. (If made with steak, let it also marinate overnight. See footnotes 66 and 77.) The next day, add the peas, water, vegetables, and spices into a large pot. Cook on high heat for 2 hours, or until reduced.[37] Enjoy and serve others in Christ for Christ (Matthew 25:31-46)!

1 lb split peas soaked overnight

1/2 lb cooked steak (*add at end*)

1 cup carrots and white onion

1 bay leaf and marjoram, black pepper and olive oil to taste

Thanksgiving Chili

Praise the LORD! Thanks be to God for His grace! And thank Him for supplying us with so many wonderful gifts such as beans, corn bread, and Thanksgiving time in general! This picture was taken last Thanksgiving and reminds me of a few special weeks spent with my family. We not only made this warm chili, but shared in many other warm memories as well. I feel God led me to choose this picture for the recipe not only because it reminds me of those times, but also because it is one of my first attempts at food photography. In this way, it's a 'weaker' photo. Paul, writing to the Church in Corinth says, "But God chose the foolish things of the world to shame the wise; God chose the weak things of the world to shame the strong. He chose the lowly things of the world and the despised things - and the things that are not - to nullify the things that are, so that no one may boast before him" (1 Corinthians 1:27). God came to save us from our sins; our strength cannot. We are not able to. What counts is putting faith in Him. I feel that God had me keep this picture to share this lesson, show that this book is not of my doing, and reveal how God will continue to work in us even if we stumble (2 Timothy 2:11-13). Consider how God made a lesson from this one 'weak' picture. Truly, after something is influenced by Christ, it is no longer weak, but strong in Him. I encourage all of us to Thank God, because it is awesome to thank the LORD, during Thanksgiving and every day. For every day is a Holiday, or 'holy day,' in the LORD (holy means *to be set apart*)!

2 1/2 lb raw mixed beans (*garbanzo, black, kidney, pinto, or anything you like*) soaked overnight

1/2 cup cheese (*try a mixture with pepper jack, cheddar, and other cheeses such as chevre*)

1/3 cup each of red and white onion

3 serrano peppers (*for even more heat, use some habanero*)

Red pepper, chili powder, cayenne pepper, and black pepper to taste

To make the chili, start a day in advance (a common theme for soups) and soak the beans overnight in twice the amount of water. The next day, pour the beans and soaking water into a large pot. Additionally, use about 1/2 cup of new water to cook with. Add the other ingredients and set to a medium-high heat. Simmer for about 2 hours (until the chili has reduced to the desired viscosity, or *thickness*) stirring well at the end. If the beans needs more time, or the chili is to thick, add a little more water. When ready, garnish and remember to Thank the LORD for His kindness. Also, if you think you're too weak, or not good enough, consider Moses, who thought that he was not good at speaking. God used Him to lead the whole Israelite nation to the Promised Land! (Exodus-Deuteronomy)[†38]

Vegetable Chicken Soup

You'll notice that the next three recipes are very repetitive! That is, they contain elements of repetition along with slight variation. The usage is modelled after the Bible's, where repetition denotes importance. For when the Bible was written, language was often conveyed orally rather than through writing. People commonly memorized huge portions of the Torah (first five books of the OT) and spoke to one another using these verses. Repetitive Scripture helped them to recall and reinforce essential lessons. One example of repetition that is personally meaningful is recorded in Psalm 136. This Psalm may have been a 'responsive reading' Psalm, where the group would repeat what was said.[39] It reads like this, "Give thanks to the LORD, for he is good. *His love endures forever. Give thanks to the God of gods. His love endures forever.* Give thanks to the LORD of lords: *His love endures forever*" (Psalm 136:1-3). There are 26 verses in all, and they are beautiful. I would encourage you and your family to read the Psalm in it's entirety, but here I'll share with you my favorite verse: "To the One who remembered us in our low estate *His love endures forever*" (Psalm 136:23). I read this one night after I thought I was broken beyond repair. But God offers us forgiveness in any and every situation. When we truly believe in Him and ask Him, He forgives us (John 6:37; Matthew 7:7)! Then we can be in His Presence. For some reason though, I needed His reminder: *His love endures forever.* He remembered me in my low estate. His love reached me then and it will continue to forever. His love also reaches out to you forever.

So this soup, and the other two that follow, all have a similar starting recipe. To read how they begin, see footnote 40. To make either the vegetable chicken or vegetable soup, cook the broth and 1/4 of the remaining ingredients on high heat for at least 1 1/2 hours. In the meantime, you can Praise the LORD for how He has given you His Son as a sacrifice for your sins! When the time is nearing, add some of the dark meat to the soup. After cooking for 45 minutes, start the water for the shell pasta (*orecchiette*). At boiling temperature, the pasta will take about 8 minutes. Strain, add the pasta, the reserved white beans, remaining chicken, and ingredients to the broth. Let the soup combine for another 10 minutes. Serve with basil and pepper jack cheese and remember that *His love endures forever!*

1 all natural, no salt added stewing chicken

2 long carrots and 2-3 celery stalks (*try red potatoes too*)

1 cup white onion

10 garlic cloves

Marjoram, basil, lemon, Italian seasoning, red pepper flakes, and black pepper to taste

Orecchiette, white beans, and pepper jack and basil to serve

Sopa de Mexíco

You'll notice that these three recipes are very repetitive! That is, they contain elements of repetition along with slight variation. The usage is modelled after the Bible's, where repetition denotes importance. For when the Bible was written, language was often conveyed orally rather than through writing. People commonly memorized huge portions of the Torah (first five books of the OT) and spoke to one another using these verses. Repetitive Scripture helped them to recall and reinforce essential lessons. One example of repetition that is personally meaningful is recorded in Psalm 136. This Psalm may have been a 'responsive reading' Psalm, where the group would repeat what was said.[39] It reads like this, "Give thanks to the LORD, for he is good. *His love endures forever*. Give thanks to the God of gods. *His love endures forever*. Give thanks to the LORD of lords: *His love endures forever*" (Psalm 136:1-3). There are 26 verses in all, and they are beautiful. I would encourage you and your family to read the Psalm in it's entirety, but here I'll share with you my favorite verse: "To the One who remembered us in our low estate *His love endures forever*" (Psalm 136:23). I read this one night after I thought I was broken beyond repair. But God offers us forgiveness in any and every situation. When we truly believe in Him and ask Him, He forgives us (John 6:37; Matthew 7:7)! Then we can be in His Presence. For some reason though, I needed His reminder: *His love endures forever*. He remembered me in my low estate. His love reached me then and it will continue to forever. His love also reaches out to you forever.

This soup, the previous one, and the one to follow, all have a similar starting recipe. To read how they all begin, see footnote 40. To make this Mexican inspired sopa, boil the broth and 1/4 of the remaining ingredients for 2 hours. This technique will create a more clear broth. Add the chicken and the ingredients listed on this page at the end, then let combine for about 10 minutes. I always seem to add more spice to garnish, such as serranos and red pepper, but you can make it however spicy you like. I love including this sopa because it reminds me of the food generously given to us in Ensenada. I will always remember how hospitable the families were, how hard they worked to give us huge meals, and how much they loved Christ. They truly showed us that *His love endures forever*.

1 all natural, no salt added stewing chicken

2 long carrots, 1 cup white onion and 7 garlic cloves

About 2 Tbsp fresh cilantro

1 lime and 2 serranos, with chili powder, red, cayenne, and black pepper to taste

Add cilantro, white onion, serrano and red pepper flakes to serve

Minestrone

You'll notice that the past three recipes are very repetitive! That is, they contain elements of repetition along with slight variation. The usage is modelled after the Bible's, where repetition denotes importance. For when the Bible was written, language was often conveyed orally rather than through writing. People commonly memorized huge portions of the Torah (first five books of the OT) and spoke to one another using these verses. Repetitive Scripture helped them to recall and reinforce essential lessons. One example of repetition that is personally meaningful is recorded in Psalm 136. This Psalm may have been a 'responsive reading' Psalm, where the group would repeat what was said.[39] It reads like this, "Give thanks to the LORD, for he is good. *His love endures forever.* Give thanks to the God of gods. *His love endures forever.* Give thanks to the LORD of lords: *His love endures forever*" (Psalm 136:1-3). There are 26 verses in all, and they are beautiful. I would encourage you and your family to read the Psalm in it's entirety, but here I'll share with you my favorite verse: "To the One who remembered us in our low estate *His love endures forever*" (Psalm 136:23). I read this one night after I thought I was broken beyond repair. But God offers us forgiveness in any and every situation. When we truly believe in Him and ask Him, He forgives us (John 6:37; Matthew 7:7)! Then we can be in His Presence. For some reason though, I needed His reminder: *His love endures forever.* He remembered me in my low estate. His love reached me then and it will continue to forever. His love also reaches out to you forever.

This soup, and the two before it, all have a similar starting recipe. To read how they begin, see footnote 40. To make this minestrone, or literally, *one soup,* or *that which is served,* boil the broth and 1/4 of the remaining ingredients (including all the chicken) for at least 2 hours. (Also note that the origin of the word *minestrone* is close to *minister,* or *servant,* which is what God has called us to be.[41] Jesus said, "If anyone wants to be first, he must be the very last, the servant of all" (Mark 9:35).) After the soup is getting nice and hot, add the orecchiette al dente, beans, and other ingredients, letting combine on low heat for another 20 minutes. Serve with plenty of mozzarella and basil in each bowl (this really makes it) and consider too that Jesus was a servant of all and how *His love endures forever.*[42]

1 all natural, no salt added stewing chicken

2 long carrots and 2-3 celery stalks

1 cup white onion

10 garlic cloves

Marjoram, basil, lemon, Italian seasoning, and black pepper to taste

Orecchiette and white beans with mozzarella and basil to serve

Pastas

Pâtes
Paste
Pastas

Heart e Pesto

Paste ('*pas-tay*' is the plural in Italian)

This pasta is naturally *hearty*! The rich pine nuts along with the fruity olive oil, fresh basil and zangy lemon make for a very full bite. And by grinding the pesto coarsely, the ingredients have a larger, more rustic flavor. I'd recommend testing this by simply eating it with a spoon.

This pasta is also *heart-worthy* for several reasons. Pine nuts are naturally high in protein, manganese, and antioxidants (which help to prevent heart disease and cancer). Also, eating pine nuts promotes digestive, liver and eye health.[43] These benefits help to make a person physically heathier. The most heart-worthy feature of this dish, though, is related to a personal experience. I had saved up for the expensive pine nuts over several weeks of anticipation. Then, even after I had gathered the ingredients, many obligations consumed my time for several more days. On the day that I was finally *enabled* to make the pasta, the sun was about to fade, but I was really set on getting a photo! I got the camera and tripod ready, praying the picture would convey God's love and peace to the viewer. I feel God has led me to do this in all my work. Well, as I was taking the picture and hoping to get a nice shot, I realized that my mom had been watching me. I felt pressured by her standing there and told her that I couldn't really concentrate. I can't believe how badly I felt afterwards because she had helped me gather the supplies! I apologized, but she assured me that there was no problem. This experience reminded me of how I'm thankful that Jesus offers forgiveness to us when we really wrong Him. In Matthew 9:2 Jesus says: "Take heart, son; your sins are forgiven." I was very concerned that our relationship was permanently broken. But when we truly have faith in Jesus, our sins are separated from us as far as the east is from the west![44] He is gracious and will forgive us. There is no need to worry. Sins do separate us from God, and are terrible; we should not abuse freedom (Galatians 5:13), but even guilt is paled by His blood! (Romans 8:1) His gift to us of Love, by His victory on the cross, is real and always available when we return to Him!

To make the pesto, simply pulse the ingredients in a food processor or blender. Then add to the pasta. You can also add chicken (see pgs. 72 and 77). When eating, remember to take heart in Him![45]

1 3/4 cups dry roasted unsalted pignolias (*pine nuts*)

1 cup basil

7-8 garlic cloves

1/3 cup red onion

3 Tbsp extra virgin olive oil

4 Tbsp choice extra virgin olive oil

1/2 (*a little less*) lemon

8-12 oz spaghetti or capellini

Parmesan cheese, basil, lemon and freshly ground black pepper to garnish

Spaghetti

Spaghetti with meatballs is such a classic meal. It always makes warm stomachs and happy hearts while reminding us of the last time we ate it. This is really similar to the classic stories of the Bible. When we read about God in the lives of Moses, Abraham, or Paul, our body is fed and our hearts become happy. Also, reading these classic stories builds a framework of memories, reminding us of how God has loved His people and helped us to see Him in the past. I would encourage you to read any part of the Bible, and to just keep reading for a while. Ask the LORD what He wants to teach you from the passages. Pray His Holy Spirit is with you and guides you (Luke 11:13)!

I'll share with you one of my favorite stories, found in Genesis 37-47. Joseph is sold into slavery by his brothers, and then rose into Pharaoh's favor because he trusted in the LORD. The dénouement is found in the unexpected response Joseph has to being reunited with his brothers: "So Joseph settled his father and his brothers in Egypt and gave them property in the best part of the land, the district of Rameses, as Pharaoh directed" (Genesis 47:11). Even though he started out as a slave, and was later imprisoned, Joseph was always faithful to God. When others saw his obedience and how God worked through him, Joseph was placed in charge of all Egypt. Joseph's faith provided a way for the LORD to show His authority to thousands and continue His promise with Abraham, Isaac and Jacob. Trust in Him and see what God can do through you! It may take a long time, and you'll have to ask God for patience, but it will be well worth the story.[66]

1 lb cooked spaghetti

Sauce: 12 ripe tomatoes, 1/3 cup red onion, 7 garlic cloves, 1/4 lemon, 1/2 cup olive oil, some basil, and spices to taste

Meatballs: 1 lb ground sirloin, 1/3 cup onion, 1 egg, 1/3 cup custom breadcrumbs, 7 garlic cloves, 1/4 lemon, 1 Tbsp olive oil, some basil, spices to taste, and 1 cup flour

To start the spaghetti sauce, dice the tomatoes and mix with the other ingredients in a large bowl. Add spices such as: red pepper flakes, marjoram, Italian seasoning, oregano, and black pepper. Afterwards, pour the olive oil in a pan, set to high heat, then add the tomato mixture. Reduce for 40 minutes, stirring the bottom to prevent burning (especially at the end) until thickened. To make the meatballs, take the ground sirloin, and mix in a bowl with all the ingredients except the flour. Form into 1 1/2 inch diameter balls, then coat with flour in a bowl. Place the meatballs in a pan on high heat. After all sides have seared, reduce to a low heat, add water, and place on a cover. Let steam for 20-30 minutes adding cheese on top in the last five minutes. When finished, serve with the pasta and enjoy a classic story in Him!

Triagatha Pasta with Chicken

What does 'Triagatha Pasta' mean? Let's start with how the name came about. I named the original title of the dish 'Margherita Pasta with Chicken.' I had noticed that many pizzas were named 'Margherita pizza' and came with tomatoes, basil, mozzarella and salt. I would always omit the salt, but added chicken instead, and made many other dishes this way. Out of convenience, I started to refer to all these dishes as 'Margherita.' However, after doing some research, I found that this title refers specifically to pizza. The combination of these three main ingredients came about as a special pizza preparation for Queen Margherita Teresa Giovanni. She was visiting Naples in 1889, and in honor of her visit and the colors of the Italian flag, Don Raffaele Esposito and his wife (the true pizza genius), made this famous pie.[46] This is a great story and there are many other parts to His-story. What would I do now though, since I referred to all of these dishes incorrectly? I decided to re-name them, *in the LORD*! The idea of re-naming came from the Old Testament. Names were given to a child in relation to God, but sometimes He changed them. One cool example is of Abraham, who had great faith in God. He was originally named Abram, which means *exalted father*. Later, in Genesis 17:5, God said, "No longer will you be called Abram; your name will be Abraham, for I have made you a father of many nations" (Abraham means *father of many*). This was right after God gave him and his wife, now re-named Sarah (which means *princess*), a child in very old age! God was bringing about His promise and reminded him, "I will establish my covenant with you for generations to come, to be your God and the God of your descendents to come" (Genesis 17:7). In honor of God, my once 'Margherita' has become His 'Triagatha,' which my friend Thomas helped name. In Greek, this means 'three (*tria*) good things (*agatha*)' and suggests the Holy Trinity. Hopefully, when you have this combination, you can tell people what the name means, through the Holy Spirit, and the LORD will be praised and awed as He should be! For both His Trinity and desire to be in relationship with us are amazing!

Sear the chicken for three minutes per side with garlic, spices and lemon. Reduce the heat to low, and cover to steam for 12 minutes until flaky. Serve with the 'Triagatha' and remember His Holy Name.[47]

1 lb all natural, no salt added chicken breast

1 lb spaghetti or capellini

3-4 garlic cloves, 1/2 lemon, marjoram, and oregano

2 Roma (*plum*) tomatoes

About 1/2 cup basil, but add to taste

1/2 cup freshly graded mozzarella

Senza sale, ma con il pepe nero a piacere

Jambalaya Pasta

'Jambalaya Pasta' is a spicy and mouth-watering dish straight from the bayou. The traditional Creole dish includes chicken, andouille sausage and seafood. It is often served over rice cooked in broth. This version includes chicken, shrimp and pasta, but you can be creative with your own recipe and discover what you like best. (You can easily make a sodium-free broth at home the night before. See footnote 40.) Experiment with how spicy you like it. You might need that extra kick!

In the Bible too, there are times when God's Word to us offers that 'kick,' or strong inspiration. God gives strong messages to make sure that His people are paying attention to His love. He mentions in Malachi how it will be right before His return to earth to set-up heaven. He says, "'Surely the day is coming; it will burn like a furnace. All the arrogant and every evildoer will be stubble, and that day that is coming will set them on fire,' says the LORD Almighty. 'Not a root or a branch will be left to them. But for you who revere my name, the sun of righteousness will rise with healing in its wings. And you will go out and leap like calves released from the stall. Then you will trample down the wicked; they will be ashes under the soles of your feet on the day when I do these things,' says the LORD Almighty" (Malachi 4:1-3). The wages of sin is death (Romans 6:23), but God loves us so much that He paid for that with Jesus' death. Now we can be set *free* from sin and live in Christ forever, because He rose and is victorious!

To make this bayou treat, start by marinating the chicken and shrimp for an hour to a day with 1/4 lemon, 3-4 chopped garlic cloves, and the spices to taste (try sassafras as well). Then, add the diced tomatoes into a pan with red onion, chopped garlic, olive oil and the spices. Set to high heat and reduce for about 40 minutes, stirring well. Meanwhile, prepare the meat. For the chicken, pan sear each side in olive oil on high heat for 3 minutes, then reduce the heat to low, cover, and let steam for about 12 minutes until flaky. For the shrimp, first de-shell and devein. Then cook with olive oil on high heat for 5-7 minutes, until they are pink and flaky, not rubbery. Start the pasta, and while it's boiling, mix the meat into the sauce. When the pasta and sauce are ready, combine and season to your spiciness level. Consider, too, His intense love!

1 lb raw, wild caught shrimp

1 lb all natural, no salt added chicken breast

1 lb penne rigate

7 fresh tomatoes (*diced*), adding about 1/4 cup olive oil

1/3 cup red onions

7 garlic cloves

1/2 lemon

Marjoram, chili powder, and red, cayenne and black pepper to taste

Orzo Pasta

Orzo pasta is named because of its similar appearance to barley or rice. In Italian, it means *barley*, and in Greek, which is the cultural influence of this specific recipe, *oryza* means *rice*. The pasta is usually prepared with soup, lamb or salad greens. Here, orzo is presented as part of a pasta salad. Along with the acidic tomatoes, sweet dates and lemon chicken, this summer salad will leave you in love with freshness. The recipe was adapted from several salads at *Elephants Delicatessen*, Portland, Oregon (see pg. 221). *Elephants* has become a home away from home; an afternoon oasis for my family and I. We love visiting not only because of the fresh local food, but also because of the welcoming atmosphere. Tim, the manager, and all of his staff are always so generous and gracious. It has been a blessing to come to *Elephants* for so long and to grow in lasting friendships (see Ruth; John 15:13-17; and pg. 45 on friendship).

Many of these outings to *Elephants* have been on Sundays. Although traditionally Saturday was the Sabbath (as seen by the names *Sabato* in Italian, or *Sábado* in Spanish), now Sundays are the day of rest. This honors Jesus raising from the grave on Sunday! Jesus said of the Sabbath, "The Sabbath was made for man, not man for the Sabbath" (Mark 2:27). Jesus showed that the day of rest was a gift from God to His people so that they could refresh from their normal activities and work. It also gives us a day to really listen to Him and do His good work (Isaiah 58:3-14)! Jesus desires us to listen to Him because good can come only through Him (Psalm 127:1; Ephesians 2:8-22; Mark 10:18; Luke 18:19). And His goodness and love will leave others refreshed in Him indeed.

To make the orzo pasta, boil the orzo in plenty of water for about 10 minutes. Meanwhile, start the chicken. Sear both sides on high heat for 3-5 minutes, with olive oil, lemon juice, marjoram and black pepper.[t48] Then reduce the heat, cover and steam to finish. When cooled, stir in with the other ingredients (cut the tomatoes and dates in half). Letting the salad ingredients rest in the fridge before serving and resting yourself in Him makes it merry!

1 lb orzo pasta

1 lb natural, no salt added chicken breast

1/3 cup red onions

1/3 cup each of red, yellow, green and orange bell peppers

1 cup cherry tomatoes (*variety*)[t23]

2 cups basil

1 cup pitless dates

1 Tbsp currants

1/2 lemon

3-4 garlic cloves

Extra virgin olive oil (*about 2 Tbsp*) and black pepper to taste

Pastas

The 'Enomoto Pasta' is named after our dear friends, the Enomotos, my brother's girlfriend's family. We commonly have celebrations and meals together on Holidays or birthdays. Sometimes, too, we'll get together to eat, hang out, or pray. It's important to have times when we share community with each other. Additionally, it's important to have special times set aside to remember what God has done for us. In the Old Testament, there are many Holidays that are set aside to remember how God had provided for His people. For example, there is the 'Firstfruits' day which the LORD taught Moses about. The LORD said, ". . . When you enter the land I am going to give you and you reap it's harvest, bring to the priest a sheaf of the first grain you harvest" (Leviticus 23:10b). This day was made to recognize God as the provider and bring people together in Him. There are many other Feast Days and Holy days (at least 12) mentioned throughout Leviticus as times to celebrate the LORD's Goodness together. The 'Sabbath' is a part of this too! Remember, Jesus said, "The Sabbath was made for man, not man for the Sabbath" (Mark 2:27). Jesus' words emphasize the importance of the Sabbath as a gift from God to us, a gift of time to be spent with Him. The day also frees us to listen to Him, enact His justice, and bring His love to others. (As described in Isaiah 58:2-14. These are amazing verses!) One of my favorite celebrations to read though is the 'Feast of Unleavened Bread.' For a while, I wondered why it was a common practice, and more holy, to eat bread without yeast. Then I read, "Do not eat it with bread made with yeast, but for seven days eat unleavened bread, the bread of affliction, because you left Egypt in haste - so that all the days of your life you may remember the time of your departure from Egypt" (Deuteronomy 16:3). God brought the Israelites out of Egypt after the Passover (Exodus 12), but they had to leave very quickly, so they did not have time to properly prepare bread with yeast. The bread is now a symbol of His deliverance (Exodus 12:39). This Holy day and others were made to remember specific events in which God provided. Now we have Jesus as our Lamb, or sacrifice, and we have new Holy days: Christmas, celebrating His birth; and Easter, celebrating His sacrifice and life. I would encourage all of us to bring glory to His Name during *Christ*mas, Easter and Thanksgiving, and have times with family that are set apart to honor and thank Him for He is amazing.

This recipe is a little different. It would be great if you could make a meal with your friends or family and use ingredients that remind you of what God has done in your life! Have fun in Him!

Create your own special pasta to remember what God has done in your life!

Pastas

Now you can have your cake and eat it too. In this sense, you can have fun making rice cakes, and get the benefit of additional healthy ingredients. Although, the metaphor is really about being in Christ! God sent His Holy Spirit to live in us forever. Paul, an apostle (from the Greek, *apóstolos* or literally, *one who is sent*) of Christ Jesus writes, "Do you not know that your body is a temple of the Holy Spirit, who is in you, whom you have received from God? You are not your own; you were bought at a price. Therefore honor God with your body" (1 Corinthians 6:19-20). Before Jesus returned to heaven for a while, He promised the Holy Spirit to be with all of us. He told His disciples, "When the Counselor comes whom I will send to you from the Father, the Spirit of truth who goes out from the Father, he will testify about me. And you also must testify, for you have been with me from the beginning" (John 15:26-27). Therefore, it is not by our own effort that we have the Holy Spirit, it is rather by *allowing* Him to live in us, so we can share Him with others (Romans 9:16). Jesus said, "Therefore go and make disciples of all nations, baptizing them in the name of the Father and of the Son and of the Holy Spirit, and teaching them to obey everything I have commanded you. And surely I am with you always, to the very end of the age" (Matthew 28:19-20). I've mentioned these verses a couple of times because of how beautiful they are! Jesus wants to establish His kingdom on earth as it is in heaven, in Him. *However, we should already experience His kingdom in us now* (Luke 17:21) and share Him with others until He does come again. For truly, He is coming again! (Revelation 22)

To make the rice cakes, first wash the rice. Afterwards, put into a large pot (or rice maker) with twice the amount of water. Cover and let simmer for 10-15 minutes. When finished, combine with the other ingredients in a large bowl. (To make the custom breadcrumbs, mince some bread, or put it diced into a blender.) Take the whole mixture and shape into some 3 1/2 inch cakes. Pat with flour on a plate and sear each side for 3 minutes over high heat. Reduce the heat, cover and let steam until complete. *Enjoy your God now and forever too!*

3 final cups cooked brown rice (*nutrition: pg. 17*)

2 cups custom bread-crumbs

3 eggs (*or try yogurt*)

1/2 Tbsp flour

2 Tbsp white onions

4 Tbsp green onions

3 Tbsp cilantro

1/4 lemon

1/2 lime

2/3 cup pepper jack cheese (*cheese optional due to high salt content*)

1 Tbsp Parmesan cheese

Crushed marjoram leaves, red pepper flakes and black pepper to taste

Fish and Seafood

Poissons et Fruits de Mer
Pesce e Frutti di Mare
Pescados y Mariscos

After reading Luke 9:10-17, I was so inspired and felt led to make this great meal of bread and fish. The fish has just olive oil, bay leaves, some cumin and pine nuts inside. It was broiled on both sides for about 7 minutes. This verse stuck out to me because of how simple and yet amazing it is. Jesus feeds five thousand people by breaking five loaves of bread and two fish. It is really a testament to how He broke His body for us and can feed so many people. Also, it's amazing that Jesus was so caring for people's needs. His apostles had just returned from a long missionary journey. Jesus was probably eager to hear from them and encourage them, "and they withdrew by themselves to a town called Bethsaida, but the crowds learned about it and followed him. He welcomed them and spoke to them about the kingdom of God, and healed those who needed healing" (Luke 9: 10-11). Jesus could have been tired or upset by the crowds, but instead of neglecting other's needs and putting His first, He served others and cared for their needs. I look at this and realize that in Christ I can serve others, but not out of my own strength. When I'm with God, He can love others through me forever and completely, rather than me trying to love them by myself! This has been revealed to me in so many ways since I first read this passage. God's love is unconditional and always available! I love the last verse too, in Luke 9:17, where it says, "They all ate and were satisfied, and the disciples picked up twelve basketfuls of broken pieces that were left over."

This meal is a perfect example of how we should have all meals: in faith! Jesus showed His disciples, and many others, how faith is the key to helping people in Him. This was the case both then and now. God still gives us daily miracles, and in Him we can share His love with all. Jesus also modelled how we get to thank our Father for meals, during grace, and for *anything*. This is true because God gives us everything! (And you might notice that I don't include serving sizes in the recipes. That is because I know God will always provide enough for you in Him!)

To make the meal, start by creating a slit in the fish's stomach. Put the spices and olive oil deep into the cavity (you can also make slits along the outside of the fish, and place seasoning and olive oil inside there). Afterwards, set the fish in a pan, and broil at 500°F for about 7 minutes. Turn to the other side and repeat. Enjoy His love and His daily provision. Amen!

5 loaves of bread

2 fish

About 1/4 cup olive oil

A few bay leaves

Cumin to taste

1 Tbsp pine nuts

Faith in Him!

Pasta ai Gamberetti

Pesce e Frutti di Mare

Shrimp is definitely one of my go-to food items. In the 'Salade aux Crevettes et Herbes,' or *Shrimp Salad with Herbes* on pg. 48, there is information on why shrimp is healthy for you. Here, though, I'll just say it's so delightful. God has given us many good things, and it is important to pause and simply thank Him for His grace.

In life, too, there are go-to things. It would be great if we all went to Jesus and read His Word, realizing that it is truly life-giving. In fact, in Paul's letter to Timothy, he writes, "But as for you, continue in what you have learned and have become convinced of, because you know those from whom you learned it, and how from infancy you have known the holy Scriptures, which are able to make you wise for salvation through faith in Christ Jesus. All Scripture is God-breathed and is useful for teaching, rebuking, correcting and training in righteousness, so that the man of God may be thoroughly equipped for every good work" (2 Timothy 3:14-17). Paul was encouraging Timothy that although there are always hard times in life, and people go astray, one must continue to listen to God's Word. Also, by living out God's Word, the Holy Spirit in us keeps us from going astray, and He helps others through us, by showing what His love and life looks like! God and His Scripture should be a go-to source for listening, loving and learning in this life. When we read God's Word, let's pray that His Holy Spirit speaks to and teaches us what He has for us that day. And let's pray that He guides our living for Him, to love Him and others more (Matthew 22:37-40)!

To make this shrimp pasta, start by selecting some wild caught, uncooked shrimp (blue in color). Then de-shell and devien. Toss into a pan with olive oil, 1/2 lemon, and spices. Sear the shrimp on high heat until light pink and flaky, not rubbery. Add the garlic to finish and toss with basil. Also, to make the dish look really gourmet, butterfly the shrimp. Simply make a small cut along the backside prior to cooking and when the shrimp meets the heat it will puff out and be quite ripe. To make the pasta, give about 15 minutes of time. When serving, also toss with Parmesan cheese, basil, and if desired, a little more lemon. Remember that Christ Jesus loves you and has so much to tell you and others through His Word. Go to Him first!

1 lb raw, wild caught shrimp (*about 25 large shrimps*)

1 lb spaghetti (*little strings*) or capellini (*angel hair*)

About 1/2 lemon

5-7 garlic cloves

1/3 cup fresh basil

Parmesan cheese flakes

Marjoram leaves, rosemary, red pepper flakes, olive oil and freshly ground black pepper to taste

Salmon

For my mother's birthday this last summer, our family enjoyed a great day in Portland. During the afternoon, we visited some of her most loved spots and in the evening, we retired to make this delicious dinner (and share favorite Bible verses). This ensemble is one of my mom's all time favorites. In fact, she almost always mentions salmon or asparagus when asked, "What do you think we should have for dinner?" And, she really prefers the steamed preparation for the salmon, while pan searing the asparagus with olive oil, garlic and pepper. The rest of us have our own beloved spots or favorite meals, but we knew that she would really appreciate us putting her desires over our own. After all, the rest of the time it seems that she is doing that for us! She ended up loving the meal and we all continued to talk about what a memorable day we had together.

The day turned out great for her and the rest of us, I'm sure, because of Jesus! He gave us time together in Him and that is all that really matters. Her birthday was also very special and different than a normal day because we put her interests first, in Christ, rather than our own. The verses in Philippians 2:4-11 describe how we should be like Jesus, who considered Himself a servant of all. Verses 4-7 say, "Each of you should look not only to your own interests, but also to the interests of others. Your attitude should be the same as that of Christ Jesus: Who, being in very nature God, did not consider equality with God something to be grasped, but made himself nothing, taking the very nature of a servant, being made in human likeness. . . . " Jesus' example is beautiful. He will encourage us to act like Him through the Holy Spirit whom He freely gives us (John 15:26).[t49] Try reading the rest and live for others, in Jesus, for Jesus (Matthew 25:31-46)!

To make the salmon, place the de-boned fillets skin side down in well-oiled cast iron pan and season lightly with lemon, oregano, red pepper and black pepper. Sear for about 4 minutes. Then cover, reduce the heat and let steam to finish. In the last 3 minutes of cooking, place the pepper jack or bleu cheese on top to melt.[t50] Mmm. To make the asparagus, see pg. 36. To make the potatoes, first chop in half, then boil in plenty of water for about 1 hour. Put the hot potatoes into a frying pan and add olive oil, lemon, oregano, red pepper, and black pepper (try thyme and rosemary as well). Sear on a medium-high heat for about 10 minutes until slightly charred. Serve with basil, garlic and others in heart (Mark 12:20-31)!

1 lb Chinook salmon[t33]

1/3 cup pepper jack or bleu cheese

2 lb red potatoes

1/4 cup fresh basil

1 bunch of asparagus

Lemon to taste (about 1)

Garlic, slivered almonds, olive oil, and spices to taste

Shrimp Pizza

Fish and Seafood

A record of the gathering of eating shrimp pizza according to Nathan the son of Dan, the son of Robert: Jordan, Emily, Alex, Nate, Jay, Inge, Daniel, Sosi, Chach, Ben, Jake, Matt, Pecos, Katie, James, Hillary, Maddie, Allyson, Lynne and Rebecca (Korinne was out of town). These were the people at the dinner/ wine tasting in Santa Barbara. Chach did not have any wine. The Portland dinner guests: Thomas, Heather, Joey, Tim, Nick Woods, whose brother is Nathan, and Maria Enomoto (Lyle and Heather had previous dinner arrangements). If there were any others, they should be honored, and many more would have been invited if they were nearby.

The above record of the people, who were in attendance at the shrimp pizza dinners, may seem a bit strange! It is modelled after the Old Testament way of recording people. To learn more about this model genealogy from Matthew 1:1-17 read footnote 51 and pg. 114.

To make the shrimp pizza, start with the dough. Mix the ingredients with just enough warm water until floury, but not sticky. Set aside for 1 hour to let rise, using a double colander.[52] Then, start the pizza sauce. Dice the tomatoes and add the olive oil, minced garlic, and spices: marjoram, oregano, Italian seasoning, thyme, red pepper flakes, olive oil and black pepper (you can also add some basil). Let it reduce in a large pan for about 40 minutes on high heat, stirring well, until thick and viscous (it is just the same as the spaghetti sauce without red onions, pg. 71). While a friend is stirring, you can thank God for pizza, preheat the oven and baking stone to 425°F, and start to de-shell and devein the shrimp. Cook the shrimp on high heat with olive oil, lemon and spices until flaky, not rubbery. Finally, prepare the other ingredients to top the pizza. Once everything is ready, take the pizza dough out and shape it into a thick circle over parchment paper. Add just enough flour to keep from sticking and do not knead or else it will become too tough! Either toss, or flatten out with a rolling pin. When formed, spoon on the sauce and add toppings to your preference. Cut the parchment paper around the pizza's edge and slide it along with the pie into the oven (make sure there's ample flour on the shovel). Bake for about 20 minutes until golden. Reserve the basil for sprinkling at the end and sit down for a wholesome meal with your friends in Jesus!

Per Pizza Pie:

Dough:
1 1/2 cups flour, 1 tsp yeast, 1 1/2 Tbsp olive oil, 1/2 lemon, and start with 1/2 cup warm water

Pizza Sauce:
4 tomatoes, 4 garlic cloves, 1/4 lemon, spices, and 1/4 cup olive oil

Toppings:
1/4 lb wild caught shrimp, 1/3 fanned red onion, 1/4 green pepper, 7 whole garlic cloves, 1 cup fresh mozzarella, 1/3 cup Parmesan when done, and olive oil, basil and red pepper to taste

Bouillabaisse

Bouillabaisse was one of the biggest and most labor-intensive meals God helped me make for this book! It took my whole family to help and was a great weekend event. My family was so blessed to make it at the Liggett's beach house, one of my favorite places, and loved being there to spend time working together on this and other projects. And working together is just what the seafood does! My friend Louie Olivares told me that poor French fishermen made bouillabaisse as a 'bottom of the bucket' solution to an end of the day's catch.[53] It is beautiful how something that had humble backgrounds has become so gourmet, and how it still involves creatively working together (Matthew 19:30). Praise God!

To start the bouillabaisse (a word I love to use) first select some fresh seafood at your local market. After returning home, choose your largest pot and begin to boil 7 liters of water with: at least 7 chopped tomatoes, 1 chopped carrot, 1 shallot, 1 Tbsp cilantro, 7-8 garlic cloves, 1/2 cup dry white wine, the juice of 1 lemon, 1/2 cup olive oil, and spices to taste (in order of concentration: about four sprigs of thyme, oregano, crushed red pepper, black pepper, chili powder and cayenne pepper)! Let this boil for about 1 1/2 hours. Meanwhile, prepare the other ingredients, so that you can add as you go, and then begin the seafood. Start with the clams or mussels. First, discard any that are already opened. Wash the remaining in cold water and then place them in a covered pan to steam. Add 1 Tbsp green onions, 1 Tbsp basil, 1/3 cup white wine, 1/2 lemon, 1 Tbsp olive oil, 1/2 cups water and red and black pepper. Give them about 5-7 minutes on high heat until opened, and discard any that do not. Set the rest aside in a double colander[52] or warm container. Then begin the salmon (if you would like, you could have someone start the next seafood in the meantime). Place the salmon in an olive oil-laden pan and fry with garlic, lemon, marjoram and . . . (To continue, look at footnote 54. I know, it is too large, but I can't leave something out!)

1 lb clams or mussels

1/2 lb salmon[33]

1 lb scallops

1 1/2 lb fresh prawns

5-7 crab legs

At least 7 tomatoes

2 long carrots

1 shallot, 4 green onions, and 1/2 cup red onion

3-4 Tbsp cilantro and basil (+ *some for garnishing*)

1 serrano pepper

About 2 heads of garlic

2 cups dry white wine

3 lemons and 1 lime

At least 2 cups extra virgin olive oil

3/4 cup mozzarella cheese

Oregano, thyme (*try sprigs too*), rosemary, marjoram, red pepper flakes, cayenne pepper, chili powder, and black pepper

Pan seared garlic bread

Fish and Seafood

This picture, the Bouillabaisse's, and the chapter header's, were all taken at the Liggett's beach house. Their beach house is by far one of my favorite places to be and gives me some of my most peaceful memories of being with God and my family. I can remember the beautiful wide beaches, their colors, the smells of the ocean, sandy feet, and the Mexican restaurant's spicy habanero salsa. I always find strength in the LORD by going there in my mind with Him in my heart.

The beach was also a perfect place to make seafood for this cookbook. My family went down to the local grocery store and got some fresh 'fruits from the sea.' We made this recipe and the bouillabaisse all at the same time, because we were there just for the night. This was such a fun evening, thanks to God and the Liggetts![155] Mind you, it was busy, but didn't seem so at the beach!

The structure of clams and shrimp hold a great lesson that fits with my memories of being with God and family at the beach. Their outer shells protect them from the powerful maritime conditions. The outer shell or protection from God is similar, and yet unique, in that it not only protects, but is joy! This *strength* is evident when at the beach in my head, or on vacation. "Nehemiah said, 'Go and enjoy choice food and sweet drinks, and send some to those who have nothing prepared. This day is sacred to our Lord. Do not grieve, for the joy of the LORD is your strength'" (Nehemiah 8:10). Let us grow in memories of times with God just as we would our loved ones. Let us hold on to these as reminders that He is our strength and shield. And let us give thanks! The Psalmist David writes, "The LORD is my strength and my shield; my heart trusts in him, and I am helped. My heart leaps for joy and I will give thanks to him in song" (Psalm 28:7).[156]

To make this light summertime recipe, start by de-shelling and deveining the shrimp, discarding any clams (or mussels too) that are already opened and rinsing both in cold water. Then, sear the shrimp on high heat for about 7-10 minutes with half of the ingredients except for basil (adding garlic at the end). They will be done when pink and flaky. For the clams, use the rest of the ingredients and steam for 5-7 minutes until opened, discarding any that remain closed. Serve with fresh basil and olive oil. Enjoy finding strength in His wonderful fruit of joy that He freely gives you! God bless your Holidays at the sea![157]

1 lb raw, wild caught shrimp

1 lb wild caught clams or mussels

2/3 cup dry white wine

1 lemon

1/3 cup fresh basil

7-8 garlic cloves

Marjoram, oregano, thyme, rosemary, red pepper flakes, chili powder, olive oil and fresh black pepper

Fish and Seafood

1/2 lb fresh crab meat

2/3 cup custom bread-crumbs

1/4 cup nonfat plain yogurt

1 large egg

1 cup cheese (*for a small kick use pepper jack*)

1 1/2 Tbsp red onion

2 green onions

1 Tbsp cilantro

1 Tbsp mustard

1 tsp serrano

3 garlic cloves

2 limes (*reserve some wedges for garnish*)

1 lemon

1 Tbsp extra virgin olive oil

1 pinch of cayenne

Red pepper to taste

Fresh black pepper to taste

Crab cakes are definitely one of my favorite treats! Also, for this book, I had quite a fun time making them. My brother and I were set on this job one bright summer evening. Before starting, we thought it would be wise to pray, as the crab was rather expensive and we desired to make it just right. Plus, we prayed that we would have a fun time. Now, can you imagine what happened? We had a blast, and these turned out just right! I honestly just put in the amounts I felt God was directing me to. This following verse describes what I know happened and is a key to living in Christ and receiving His promises. Jesus said, "If you believe, you will receive whatever you ask for in prayer" (Matthew 21:22). I thought, "If I believe He can make them turn out, then He will." This is also the case with anything. We should, ". . . pray in the Spirit on all occasions with all kinds of prayers and requests. With this in mind, be alert and always keep on praying for all the saints" (Ephesians 6:18).[58] We can come to Jesus with any prayer! It is important, though, to have the same goals and heart that He does. For example, if we are praying for someone to be healed and set free from their suffering, it will work if it is God's will. It might take a while, but He is at work. However, if we are praying for our greed, then it will be against God's will. This is a common problem, for, "When you ask, you do not receive, because you ask with wrong motives, that you may spend what you get on your pleasures" (James 4:3). So, from small to large miracles, just have faith in Him for Him, and His love on earth will be made known to all people (Matthew 21:21)![59]

To make the crab cakes, take your fresh crab meat with all the ingredients and work together in a large bowl. Add custom breadcrumbs by mincing some bread, or putting it diced into a blender. Take handfuls of the mixture and shape into a few 3 1/2 inch cakes. Pat with flour on a plate and then sear each side for about 3 minutes on high heat. Reduce the heat, cover and let steam for about 7 minutes until complete. I would encourage you to pray about anything, even crab cakes; I know you'll find God right there with you! (Matthew 7:7-11)

Steak and Poultry

Viande et Volaille
Bistecca e Pollame
Carne y Avícolas

This recipe is actually titled 'Kale-Steak' and was the first recipe made for the He Art cookbook. In honor of this inaugural recipe and pg. 101, here is an introduction to that day and a '101' on the He Art cookbook making process (for the full recipe from that day, look at footnote 60)!

So this 'Kale-Steak' meal came about after a fine day spent with my friend Josh Tengan. Josh and I had visited our organic community garden at Westmont College. He had arranged to meet our friend Shannon there, a volunteer at the garden, who helped donate some of the produce locally. It was a nice sunny afternoon and we all enjoyed tending to God's creation. Right before leaving, Shannon kindly offered us some fresh kale. Well, of course we received it with joy! After returning home and approaching dinner time though, we were wondering what to make with it. Being that we were in Santa Barbara and close to a local *bodega* (Spanish for *corner market*),[61] we thought why not try it with some marinated asada? This seems as odd now as it did at that point, but we were feeling hopeful. At *Mi Fiesta Grill*, we purchased some freshly marinated asada and Josh inquired about what we would have to drink with this unique concoction. To follow suit, he suggested a $1.50 white wine. This meal was turning out to be the biggest fusion recipe I have enjoyed eating. When we returned home, we caramelized the onions and kale in a giant wok, giving an Asian inspiration to it all. Then, after adding the asada and some orange juice to tie it together, we reduced the heat to finish. With humorous anticipation, we sat down and had *one of my favorite meals ever!* We were simply amazed at how it tasted so great. Really, this is a fine tastin' meal, and the white wine goes with it so well! To our semi-suprise and post-satisfaction, we would both recommend this recipe to you, and trying new things in Christ!

That afternoon was very entertaining and enjoyable. I'm glad that we were filled with Christ's love and peace *to enjoy it all*. It may seem strange that I add Christ, but really it starts with Christ and how He first loved us (John 3:16-17)! From Him, then we are all enabled to appreciate His beauty and love in everything else. This is why I started each page's template with 'Jesus Loves.' Also, anywhere there could be text, it would start as 'Jesus Loves.' That was done to remind Who this cookbook is for, and to give you His Love and Truth, not my own. He is the One who has inspired this cookbook from this recipe forward and every good thing ever! I pray that we all hear God speaking to us for He has so much good to say and accomplish. Let's trust in Him, no matter what, and serve others in Him and for Him with whatever gifts He gives us! (Matthew 25:31-46)[62] Amen!

Chicken Pot Pie

Chicken pot pie is one of my dad's favorite meals. I definitely agree that it's very hearty and healthy in theory. However, I find that I don't eat it often because of the salty chicken broth and high fat content.[63] Well, here is a solution at last! There is neither salt, butter, nor shortening! Now the whole family can eat my dad's favorite.

This meal was quite a challenge though. It took a few tries and several weeks to get a crust that would taste nice and be strong enough without the fat. I have to say that it's just not the same as a finely made pie with shortening, but it *is* a healthy alternative. I'm thankful that God gave me this option. As I recall making it and being frustrated with how hard it was, I realize that my hardships don't even compare with those of some of my neighbors. Many people daily don't have enough food or water. Let's help our neighbors and anyone we meet with Christ's love in us. Let's provide them with what they need both physically and emotionally, and let's tell them about Jesus who is the way, the truth and the life (John 14:6)! Here are a few verses that go along with these thoughts. In John 16:33 Jesus says, "I have told you these things, so that in me you may have peace. In this world you will have trouble. But take heart! I have overcome the world." I would also recommend reading the preceding verses, Isaiah 1:17-20, Isaiah 58:5-12, Matthew 25:31-46, and James 2:14-26. Remember, too, that it may not be their fault they don't have things. Just read Job's story.

Pie: 1 sweet potato, 3 apples, 3 cups flour, 1 lb cooked chicken, 2/3 cup broccoli, 1/3 cup yellow onions, 1/2 cup carrots, 1 cup parsnips, 3-4 garlic cloves, 1/4 cup peas and 1/3 cup cheese

Sides: 2-3 Baker (*Russet*) potatoes with 2 green onions, 1/4 carrot, 3-4 garlic cloves, olive oil, 1/4 cup milk, and 3/4 lb green beans [77]

Marjoram, oregano, thyme, basil, olive oil and black pepper

To make the pie, I would give yourself an afternoon or a day in advance. Begin with the crust. Dice all the potatoes and boil each type in separate pots. With the Russets, add olive oil and the spices (try a bay leaf as well). After softened, strain and set aside. Then purée 1/3 cup of the sweet potato and 1 cup of the apple, reserving the rest just for snacking! Mix with 3 cups flour, and about 1 Tbsp warm water, until the dough is flowery, but not sticky. Cut off slightly more than half of the dough to roll out for the bottom. Rub the inside of a pie pan with olive oil and then transfer the dough (see footnote 64). Meanwhile, preheat the oven to 350°F, and fill the pie. Place the top on and cut some slits for ventilation.[64] Brush with milk and bake for 30 minutes. Serve with the mashed potatoes garnished with basil, green beans, and letting Christ's love shine![65]

Tacos de Carne Asada

Steak tacos are simple masterpieces. You can easily taste many years of tradition and flavor within every small bite. And I love all steak tacos, but *especially* appreciate the authentic ones I've had in Ensenada, Mexico. In fact, I have tried many times to replicate these works of art, but this means many failed attempts (it has been fun to try though). They are indelibly delicious!

More than the tacos from Ensenada, which are hard to beat, I have enjoyed the relationships God has given me from there. Whenever I visited, so many people that I met were truly kind. They welcomed us into their homes and gave us their food to eat. It is not uncommon too, that the mothers would get up early in the morning and spend all day making this delicious food! Plus, whenever we ate, the amount was always more than enough. We would come back for seconds and thirds, sometimes even more, and still there was some of the best left over (John 2:1-11). I can't express how thankful and moved I feel for their kindness and generosity, not just in food, but more so in His Spirit. God has taught me much through their culture. I was impressed indelibly.

Visiting Mexico taught me about true service. The people there truly served us. They did not do so just in speech, but in heart and action. Let's also love people with God's heart and action. Remember the verse in Ezekiel 11:19 when God says, "I will give them an undivided heart and put a new spirit in them; I will remove from them their heart of stone and give them a heart of flesh." Following God's lead, trust in Him and serve with your new heart!

To start the tacos, select your steak: choose a thin and lean cut. Marinate at home for an hour to a day with red onions, cilantro, chopped garlic, lime juice, all the spices and olive oil. Then take the steak and sear both sides on a grill set to high heat for about 5 minutes. Reduce the heat and let finish for 5 more minutes on each side (the inside temperature should be about 150°F for medium rare, 160°F for medium and 170°F for well done). Finally, cover with tin foil and set on the counter to rest for 7 last minutes. It will end up well cooked, but still pink![t66] In the meantime, chop up all the ingredients and set in bowls to serve. Also, get some guacamole going and place parchment paper in a basket for salt-free chips. Don't forget to serve with warmed corn tortillas (less salt than flour) and singleness of heart for Him!

1 lb marinated carne asada or thinly cut top sirloin

Plenty of corn tortillas

1 red onion, 2 tomatoes, 1 cup fresh cilantro, 2-7 garlic cloves and 3-4 limes

1 cup queso fresco or pepper jack cheese

Guacamole (*see pg. 121*)

Red pepper flakes, chili powder, cayenne pepper, and serrano peppers to taste

Chicken Tacos

In the beginning of this cookbook was this picture, and the picture was with God. The picture was with God in the beginning of the cookbook.

This recipe and the one before it are linked. The one before helped to prepare the way for this one. (There are actually a few recipes like this pair. Can you find all three of them?) The previous recipe talked about how tacos related to my experience in Mexico. It focused on service, and what Jesus said in Mark 10:43-45: "Not so with you. Instead, whoever wants to become great among you must be your servant, and whoever wants to be first must be a slave of all. For even the Son of Man did not come to be served, but to serve, and to give his life as a ransom for many." Jesus served us! The Gospel of Mark focuses on service and how we should be like Christ, actually re-giving the love that He gives to us. The previous recipe was like the Gospel of Mark.

This recipe started like the Gospel of John. It focused on how God already had this picture ready before I knew about it (when I saw it, I just knew that it was the cover picture), and helped pave the way for the rest of the cookbook. The disciple John wrote about how Jesus saves and paved the Way (see John 1:1-7,14, and 14:6)! John's account of the Gospel can be simplified in John 3:16: "For God so loved the world that he gave his one and only Son, that whoever believes in him shall not perish but have eternal life."[67] All four Gospels are written by different people, and reflect the light of Jesus in a personal way. To read more information on the Gospel writers, see footnote 67, which includes commentary from my Bible. Let's all try to read through the Gospels on a day-to-day basis, and come to know Jesus more and more fully, for He knows us fully! (1 Corinthians 13:12-13 and preceding verses. Also, see John 3:17!)

To make the chicken tacos, start with the chicken! Marinate with all the spices, red onions, cilantro, limes and olive oil an hour to a day in advance. Then sear the chicken on high heat with some more olive oil. After about 5 minutes, reduce the heat, cover and let steam until complete. Shred with two forks, pulling the chicken apart. Add more lime juice and prepare bowls filled with the fresh ingredients. To make the tortillas more authentic (remember, corn variety have less salt than flour), oil and stack over a heated pan. Flip and rotate until golden-brown. Then share with others *your* Gospel account of Jesus![68]

1 lb all natural chicken breast

1 red onion, 2 tomatoes, 1 cup cilantro, 1/2 cucumber, 2-7 garlic cloves, 3-4 limes, 1 cup queso fresco/ pepper jack, and plenty of corn tortillas

Guacamole (see pg. 121)

Chili powder and red, cayenne and serrano pepper to taste

Rocoto Relleno

God gave me the great opportunity to first enjoy rocoto relleno in Cusco, Peru. My friends Jordan Johnson, Alex Job, Chachie Hernandez, Jordan Evans and I were visiting our college friend Marcos Paredes Sadler, who grew up in Lima. During one crisp evening at dinner, I found that I literally had my breath taken away. This is because of the high elevation in Cusco, but also because of how spicy this dish was. Rocoto relleno means *stuffed rocoto*, and as I discovered, rocoto is a very spicy pepper. It looks like a common bell pepper, but has as much capsaicin as a habanero (capsaicin is the chemical that produces the sensation of spice)![t69] As I was sitting there with all of my layers on, I remember becoming very hot. When I returned home, I tried to make this dish again because I love pure heat! I thought that I would just add some serranos or spices to the steak and use a bell pepper. The results were of course not the same. Then I looked up rocoto and found the answer. Before, I was just looking at the outside of the pepper. The heart is what counted.

Jesus also has a similar teaching, but one that is much more important. He says to the hypocrites who thought they were saved because of their external deeds: "Woe to you, teachers of the law and Pharisees, you hypocrites! You clean the outside of the cup and dish, but inside they are full of greed and self-indulgence. Blind Pharisee! First clean the inside of the cup and dish, and then the outside also will be clean" (Matthew 23:25-26). Jesus wants our hearts, souls, minds and strengths to be genuinely for Him. Jesus said the greatest commandment was to, "Love the Lord your God with all you heart and with all your soul and with all your mind and with all your strength" (Mark 12:30). It is not what we do, but rather living fully for Jesus that matters. Only then can we have a more *pure*, or devoted flavor.[t70]

To make the rocoto relleno, it would be nice to have the real deal, but rocotos are hard to find in the States![t71] Using bell peppers with spicy serranos/ habaneros is a great alternative, as long as your heart is for Jesus! First take the marinated steak and sear both sides on high heat for 5 minutes. Then reduce the heat to finish.[t66] Mix with all the ingredients in a bowl and generously stuff the peppers (cut the tops diagonally, so they don't cave in). Oil the peppers and place on pie tins over high heat for 10 minutes or until slightly charred.[t73] Get a glass of milk and remember the heart of purity![t70]

7 rocotos or bell peppers

1 lb freshly marinated steak

1 cup cooked quinoa [t72]

1/3 cup red onions, 10 garlic cloves, 1 serrano, 1/3 habanero (*optional*), 1 cup pepper jack cheese, cilantro, and 1 lime

Red and cayenne pepper, chili powder, and olive oil to taste

Steak and Vegetable Shish Kebabs

The name 'shish kebab' means *roast meat* (kebap) on a *skewer* (sis).[74] The Turkish treat comes in many different varieties and in my home, making this version has become a family favorite. In fact, whenever I think of summer during childhood, I recall barbecuing some kebabs.

Kebabs come up in many other culture's cuisines as well. This version is very Americanized, but I have also enjoyed kebabs with Asian combinations, such as hot sauce and rice, and have tried Mediterranean yogurt-marinated chicken kebabs (a recipe from my friend Jordan Johnson). In Italy, too, I noticed that there were many kebabs being sold, and you can really find variations of them anywhere. This culturally ubiquitous meal reminded me of how we should be towards one another in Christ. Paul, an ambassador of Christ, wrote to the Corinthian Church, "Though I am free and belong to no man, I make myself a slave to everyone, to win as many as possible. To the Jews I became like a Jew, to win the Jews. To those under the law I became like one under the law (though I myself am not under the law), so as to win those under the law. To those not having the law I became like one not having the law (though I am not free from God's law but am under Christ's law), so as to win those not having the law. To the weak I became weak, to win the weak. I have become all things to all men so that by all possible means I might save some" (1 Corinthians 9:19-22). Paul was not being tricky, he was just being culturally relevant. Consider, if we visit a country and think that our ways are the best, then we miss the people there. Anywhere we are, let's live with Christ in us, to listen to others needs. In doing so, Jesus can teach all of us and we will all learn more about His Law, not our own culturally biased one. Remember which commandments Jesus said all of the Law and Prophets hang on: "Jesus replied, 'Love the Lord your God with all your heart and with all your soul and with all your mind.' This is the first and greatest commandment. And the second is like it: 'Love your neighbor as yourself.' All of the Law and the Prophets hang on these two commandments'" (Matthew 22:37-40)! Jesus is about love!

To make the kebabs, first decide on your cultural influence and flavor accordingly. These kebabs are marinated in these spices and olive oil for an hour to a day. Then skewer with your meat and/ or vegetable choices. Cook on a barbeque set to at least 500°F for 10 minutes, rotating until finished to your liking (remember, metal skewers get very hot). Enjoy His depth in His food and people![75]

2 lb marinated steak or poultry

Vegetables: cherry tomatoes,[23] bell peppers, onions, mushrooms and more (*try zucchini as well*)

Red and black pepper, garlic cloves, marjoram and olive oil

Steak and Potatoes

As steak and potatoes are to our stomachs, so should God's Word should be to our hearts. Seriously, do you ever crave protein, bread, potatoes, or something filling? Consider Psalm 63:1: "A *psalm of David. When he was in the Desert of Judah.* O God, you are my God, earnestly I seek you; my soul thirsts for you, my body longs for you, in a dry and weary land where there is no water." We all have had this cry! Yet thank God because His Word is very filling, and His Holy Spirit freely offered to all *fills every need!* We're made for Him, so let's let Him in! (Jesus giving the Holy Spirit, or 'Counselor,' is mentioned in many places such as John 14:16, 26; 15:26, and 16:7!)

Paul writes in his first letter to the Corinthian Church that Jesus gave us bodies that were meant to be filled with His Spirit. He says, "Do you not know that your body is a temple of the Holy Spirit, who is in you, whom you have received from God? You are not your own; you were bought at a price. Therefore honor God with your body" (1 Corinthians 6:19-20). This verse has many lessons. To start, Paul is specifically speaking about being pure sexually. He describes that we have a body from Christ, for Him, so let's not sin against ourselves and God! The passage also shows only God should fill us. Think about it, if you are filled with something else, how can there be room for the Holy, or '*set apart*' God? In Revelation it is recorded, "Who will not fear you, O Lord, and bring glory to your name? For you alone are holy. All nations will come and worship before you, for your righteous acts have been revealed" (Revelation 15:4). Jesus should be the pure and undivided focus of our hearts.[170] When we seek other things to fill us, they will only leave us more void, and take away His place to fill us. He desires an undivided heart. And finally, from this verse, we can see the Holy Spirit in us is what He intended. He is who we were made for. C.S. Lewis writes in 'Mere Christianity' that, "God made us: invented us as a man invents an engine. A car is made to run on gasoline, and it would not run properly on anything else. Now God designed the human machine to run on Himself. He Himself is the fuel our spirits were designed to burn, or the food our spirits were designed to feed on. There is no other."[176] Let's honor God with our bodies by receiving Him and His Word in us! (Jesus is the Way and the Word! (John 1:14))[177]

Making the steak and potatoes, just like reading God's Word, is simple. Whatever you end up with will be really nutritious and filling. Plus, over time we realize the gourmet tastes! Read footnote 77 for a recipe and remember He alone can fill our needs!

1 lb marinated top sirloin steak

3 Russet potatoes, milk and basil

1 lb asparagus, 1/2 red onion, 4 garlic cloves, lemon, olive oil, and red and black pepper

Chicken Pizza!

Steak and Poultry

"For what the law was powerless to do in that it was weakened by the sinful nature, God did by sending his own Son in the likeness of sinful man to be a sin offering. And so he condemned sin in sinful man, in order that the righteous requirements of the law might be fully met in us, who do not live according to the sinful nature but according to the Spirit" (Romans 8:3-4). Paul explains here how Jesus is the way, the truth and the life (Jesus said this in John 14:6) and that He is the fulfilment of the Law, or regulations to be righteous. *Jesus' sacrifice is for us, so that we can have a right and righteous relationship with God!* We are set free in His Spirit! Jesus also explains, "Do not think that I have come to abolish the Law or the Prophets; I have not come to abolish them but to fulfil them. I tell you the truth, until heaven and earth disappear, not the smallest letter, not the least stroke of a pen, will by any means disappear from the Law until everything is accomplished" (Matthew 5:17-18). Jesus fulfilled all the Law's requirements and prophecies about Him, the Christ! He will also return, just as He promised, to make His righteous kingdom on earth![178] In the last pizza recipe (pg. 90), there are some 'laws' or 'recipe foundations.' This recipe fills in many gaps and shows that pizza-making is an art form for Him. We are not saved by the Law, but *only by Jesus!* Let's let Jesus live in us, to set us free by His Spirit, with cooking, art and everything![179]

For the basic recipe, see pg. 90. More specifically, start making the dough by mixing the ingredients in a bowl with a spoon. When workable, move to a well-flowered surface. With floured hands, knead the dough, adding enough flour and water until it's not sticky (try not to knead too long). Then preheat the oven and baking stone to 425°F. Meanwhile, the aroma from cooking the pizza sauce will invite many friends. With their help you can customize your pies, and talk about, and thank Him! Start by shaping the dough. I've found that it doesn't have to be perfect, and the organic shapes actually look more gourmet. Also, I like to push down with my thumbs 1-2 inches inside the edge to make the crust more pronounced. As you top the pizzas, experiment with the amount or type of cheese. Try a variety, and add some after the pizza's ready. Most of all, enjoy the freedom in Him, given to serve others for Him in love! (Galatians 5:13)[179]

Per Pizza Pie:
Dough: 1 1/2 cups flour, 1 tsp yeast, 1 1/2 Tbsp olive oil, 1/2 lemon, and 1/2 to 3/4 cups warm water until right texture

Pizza Sauce: 4 tomatoes, 4 garlic cloves, 1/4 lemon, spices, and 1/4 cup olive oil

Toppings: 1/2 lb all natural chicken breast, 1/3 red onion, 7 whole garlic cloves (*I love whole garlic cloves*), 1 cup fresh mozzarella, 1/3 cup Parmesan at end, and olive oil, basil and red pepper to taste

Jay's Spicy Enchiladas

Carne y Avícolas

I love the feeling when I've eaten some green, pulsed, serrano y habanero salsa, and then follow it with cool, limey guacamole on salt-free blue and red corn tortilla chips. The spiciness increases with every bite and the pain becomes part of the flavor. Not many people like this sensation. The only other person I've met who enjoys spice as much as I do is Jay Tagliareni. And he and his delightful wife, Inge, always make interesting and delicious culinary combinations, so I just had to get this one in. If you like spice, then these are the enchiladas for you! Of course, when Jay makes them, he also kindly offers a non-spicy portion. (Try to enjoy at least a little zip though!)

It might not be the case that you enjoy spicy food as much as Jay or I do, but there is still a lesson we can all learn together with the idea of spice in mind. In the Beatitudes, Jesus talks about the qualities of people who follow Him. These are also the qualities that will make up His kingdom.[78] When Jesus was giving these blessings at the beginning of the 'Sermon on the Mount,' He was completely changing how people currently thought. For example, Jesus says in the third Beatitude, "Blessed are the meek, for they will inherit the earth" (Matthew 5:5). Now, even for us today, who have His teaching in the Bible, this is a shocking reality! But this is true. Jesus and His promises to us are always true.[80] Each Beatitude has a similar shock and redeeming value, especially in the last one, for if we do live by it, the pain truly does become part of the flavor. Jesus said, "Blessed are those who are persecuted because of righteousness, for theirs is the kingdom of heaven" (Matthew 5:10). Acts 5:17-42 gives a very clear, real example of this verse being applied. I would encourage all of us to live for Jesus, and not relish in the occasional pain, but in Who we are living for. For He has loved, is loving, and will love us forever. He is very refreshing!

Jay's spicy enchiladas will have you coming back for more and more! To start them, prepare the chicken. Sear both sides on high heat for 3 minutes, reduce the heat, then cover to let steam until the chicken is just about done (it will finish in the oven later). Cut into pieces, add some lime juice and set aside. Next, preheat an oven to 350°F and select some tortillas (corn variety have less salt than flour). Coat the tortillas with salt-free canned, or home-made tomato sauce. Use the same . . . (See footnotes 81 and 82 for the rest!) God Bless you in living for Him!

2 1/2 lb all natural chicken breast

20-25 large tortillas

15 tomatoes, 1/2 chopped red onion, 7-8 garlic cloves, 1/2 cup fresh cilantro, 3-4 limes, unsalted sunflower seeds, and enchilada cheeses

Red pepper flakes, chili powder, cayenne pepper, 2 serrano and 1 habanero peppers, and hot sauce

Desserts

Desserts
Dolci
Postres

Guacamole

Guacamole for dessert! Is this in the right place? Well, it turns out that I actually don't eat that many desserts besides fruit and chocolate, so guacamole has become one of my favorite *treats*. But if you think about it, you can eat it before a meal, after a meal, as a late night snack, and in these ways, it's just like a dessert! Guacamole is more to me than a favorite treat, though. I love *making* this brilliant, traditional and unique food more than any other. Also, every time I do make guacamole, I'm reminded of the time before.

It is fitting then to pair my favorite and most nostalgic food recipe with my favorite and most beloved *God-recipe*, or passage of Scripture, Hebrews 12:1-29. When I first read this passage I was sitting on Hammonds Beach in Santa Barbara with my friend Ben Ingalls. I can remember stumbling upon the verse and being blown away. I'll gladly admit that afterwards, Christ showed me so much of His glory and truth (actually, *Christ does this all the time and for everyone*), only because now I care more to look. I would encourage you to read the whole passage, and also to find your own favorite passages of Scripture. Let Him use these verses to speak to your heart as direct messages from Him. And let's allow Him to continually guide us and speak to us as we look to Him in our daily walk. Here is my favorite verse to close, "Let us fix our eyes on Jesus, the author and perfecter of our faith, who for the joy set before him endured the cross, scorning its shame, and sat down at the right hand of the throne of God" (Hebrews 12:2).

To make the guacamole, first select your avocados. Find fruit that is notably soft, but not squishy, and has a darker color. When cutting into the avocado, the ripe ones have a nice, full, green-and-yellow pulp. To cut them, slice longitudinally around the pit with a knife, taking out the stem. Then lay the avocado on a cutting board and hit the pit with your knife, turning until it comes right out. With a spoon, carve out the meat. Mash slightly in a bowl and add all spices. The amounts may vary based on how ripe the avocado is and how you like them. I often find myself adding more cilantro, lime, chili powder and sometimes 1 Tbsp shallot and 1/4 of a habanero. Mix the amounts, adding your preferred ratios, until thick and pasty. Garnish and serve with salt-free chips. Remember, too, He is waiting for you! Just look!

7 medium-large, ripe Hass avocados (*green gold*)

3/4 cup red onions

4 Tbsp fresh cilantro (+*1 to garnish*)

2 garlic cloves

1 1/2 limes, 1/4 lemon

1-2 serrano peppers

1 tsp red pepper flakes, 1/2 tsp chili powder and 1/2 tsp cayenne pepper

Sue's Chocolate Oatmeal Cake*

*great for cake or cupcakes   Desserts

Decadent, dense, delicious and healthy? Yes, indeed. This is a a rich and fine chocolate cake that is actually *very* nutritious. And based in oatmeal and flour, you might be surprised at the beautiful taste, but my friend Sue Landgren, nutritionist and expert baker, has come up with quite the special gateau.

You'll notice, too, that the cake does not take that long to bake, and it is really fun to make with all of the proportions thought-out beforehand. It is begging to be eaten and enjoyed. This is the same with *all* Scripture! Paul, in his letter to Timothy explains that, "All Scripture is God-breathed and is useful for teaching, rebuking, correcting and training in righteousness, so that the man of God may be thoroughly equipped for every good work" (2 Timothy 3:16). Scripture is rich, dense and yet nutritious just like this cake. Also, it is fun to read and 'eat.' I pray that we can all look to God more through His Word and respond to His thought-out proportion and life-changing way in Jesus, who He graciously offered for us (John 14:6).

There are so many sweet passages, some that we have heard and read many times, and some that are new. Here is a newer passage to me that is so delicious. Peter, an apostle of Jesus Christ, reminds Christians of the verse in Isaiah 28:16, which says, ". . . See I lay a cornerstone in Zion, a chosen and precious cornerstone, and the one who trusts in him will never be put to shame" (1 Peter 2:6). There will be no shame for those who trust in Jesus! Praise the LORD for Him![83]

To make the cake, Sue says to first preheat an oven to 350°F and mix the wet and dry ingredients separately. Afterwards, add the wet to the dry and stir well. Bake the cake for 20-30 minutes, and test with a toothpick. If clean, the cake is ready! This recipe usually makes 12 cupcakes or one 8"x 8" cake.[84] Sue also offers some tasty variations, such as chocolate chips (try mint), raisins, and/or nuts placed in the dry ingredients' batter before baking. Here, I have added some fresh strawberries and walnuts to garnish. Now, I don't know if Sue would like this, but I also love to eat lime with chocolate cake. Whatever you find, though, there is no shame in Him![83]

Wet:

1/4 cup vegetable oil

1 Tbsp vinegar

2 tsp vanilla

1 cup cold water

Dry:

1 cup sugar

1 cup flour

1/2 cup whole wheat flour

1/2 cup quick-cooking oatmeal

1/4 cup cocoa powder

1 tsp baking soda

Toppings:

1 box fresh strawberries

8 oz crumbled walnuts

lime wedges

Rhubarbara Pie

Desserts

If you read the 'Salmon Salad' recipe on pg. 47, you would have learned that in our family, Barbara Setniker is our dear grandma figure. Barbara kindly helped raise my brother, Nick, and I when we were younger. Both of us remember taking many nature walks, hearing interesting facts and discovering more about God's love from Barbara. Most recently, we have really enjoyed her amazing garden filled with fresh strawberries, blueberries, and rhubarb. Barbara's garden truly expresses God's hand in nature.

On one of the recent occasions spent with her, we learned to make her famous rhubarb pie. Barbara is actually the best pie maker around, so we dedicated a whole afternoon to it and took many notes. Barbara explained to us how this pie developed. She recalled that one year, when her "youngest one" was still little, they were visiting someone for the Holidays. She had set aside a sauce dish full of blueberries to give her daughter. Since her daughter did not want them for some reason, and Barbara had about 15 blueberry bushes at home, there was no need to bring this small amount back with her. Without telling anyone, she just added them to the rhubarb pie. Well, everyone loved it, and ever since then, Barbara has not made a rhubarb pie without blueberries! That was about 40 years ago and Barbara makes many pies per year. Thank God for intervening in creative moments!

It is just like the taste of rhubarb when God intervenes. Sometimes, it is sweet, and sometimes more raw and seemingly tart. But after understanding Him more, we can develop a taste of His infinite goodness and mercy. Hearing about a favorite Bible verse of Barbara's made me realize this truth. She shared, 'Jesus telling the parable of the workers paid equally,' as recorded in Matthew 20:1-16. Jesus says, "For the kingdom of heaven is like a landowner who went out early in the morning to hire men to work in his vineyard. He agreed to pay them a denarius for the day and sent them to work in his vineyard." I would encourage you to read the rest and see that although we think God is sometimes being unfair, in reality, He has given us the best opportunity ever in Jesus. We just don't understand His good ways. God is for us, so let's trust in sweet Him.[t85]

Crust: 1 1/3 cups shortening (for shortening substitutes, see pg. 103), 3 cups flour, and warm water until right texture

To make this pie, practice helps! I would recommend giving yourself a whole afternoon the first time. Plus, there are actually three recipes here from Barbara! Just the first is 'Rhubarbara Pie' (see footnote 86)!

Filling: rhubarb, blueberries, and 3/4 cup sugar

Marionberry Pie

"Mmm, marionberry pie," is a common thought of mine around the Holidays. I thank God for making Holidays to help us refresh and rejuvenate in Him so that we can be better servants for others. I also thank God for providing many delicious foods and desserts during these times, including marionberries. Growing up in Oregon, I thought that they were ubiquitous, but it turns out that they are an Oregon-native hybrid of the blackberry and the raspberry! If you would like the taste, but don't have marionberries, I would suggest just combining a pie with blackberries and raspberries. I'm sure that you won't be disappointed with the result. I'm convinced that berries are some of the simplest testaments of God's handiwork.

What, then, is the best testament of God's handiwork? You may have read Romans 1:20: "For since the creation of the world God's invisible qualities - his eternal power and divine nature - have been clearly seen, being understood from what has been made, so that men are without excuse." God is revealed in nature. Think of how intricate the universe is. Why are we here?

But still, that is not the greatest testimony. People are much greater carriers of God's Word. Consider the beauty in an eye, or God's loving character expressed through His people as they look to Him in service for Him. Think also of God's call, as spoken through Jesus, "Therefore go and make disciples of all nations, baptizing them in the name of the Father and of the Son and of the Holy Spirit, and teaching them to obey everything I have commanded you. And surely I am with you always, to the very end of the age" (Matthew 28:19-20). Baptism is an outward sign of the inward grace. It is a repentance, or change in heart, to turn towards God. It is shifting our whole focus to Him. This is so Holy and only from Him.[87]

However, still, the apostle John says, "He did not need man's testimony about man, for he knew what was in a man" (John 2:25). Jesus knew that mankind needed Him to save them. Consider John 3:16. Jesus came to save us! Jesus means, *the LORD saves*. Jesus is the best testament of God's handiwork! God, fully good and all powerful, humbled Himself to enter into humanity so that people could have a relationship with Him, even deeper than a husband and wife relationship. God is what our hearts yearn for. He completes us. Jesus is God in the flesh so that we can begin to understand this real God who loves us. It is Jesus and His perfect life, finished by His perfect work of obedience by dying on a cross for us, that tells of God's handiwork. This has never before happened in history, and it tells us that He is for our love! (See footnote 86 for the recipe!)

Desserts

Fresh, ripe fruit is hard to beat. It tastes good, is extremely healthy for you, and is a gift from God. On a summer day, I'm sure you have noticed how great fruit is, and really offers the perfect dessert. We have also talked a little about how fruit is healthy for you because it has a lot of fiber (see 'An Introduction to Pasta and Carbs,' pg. 12), and know that fruit has a lot of potassium (see also 'Foods High in Potassium,' pg. 220). However, this introduction just gets the juices flowing. God has so many lessons about fruit as well.

To start, Jesus says, "Produce fruit in keeping with repentance" (Matthew 3:8). What is Jesus referring to? He is referring to the 'Fruit of the Spirit.' Paul writes to the Galatian Church, "But the fruit of the Spirit is love, joy, peace, patience, kindness, goodness, faithfulness, gentleness and self-control. Against such things there is no law. Those who belong to Christ Jesus have crucified the sinful nature with its passions and desires. Since we live by the Spirit, let us keep in step with the Spirit. Let us not become conceited, provoking and envying each other" (Galatians 5:22-26). When we remain in His Spirit, His fruit is the natural produce of our replaced hearts. Ezekiel records the LORD saying, "I will give them an undivided heart and put a new spirit in them; I will remove from them their heart of stone and give them a heart of flesh" (Ezekiel 11:19). Only with the Holy Spirit in us, is the preciously gifted fruit ripe to give to others, so that they too can hear about Him and have their hearts changed by Him. Jesus explains that He alone is the Way (John 14:6) to make fruit. He says, "Remain in me, and I will remain in you. No branch can bear fruit by itself; it must remain in the vine. Neither can you bear fruit unless you remain in me. I am the vine; you are the branches. If a man remains in me and I in him, he will bear much fruit; apart from me you can do nothing" (John 15:4-5). Through Jesus the good fruit comes, otherwise there is nothing. For example, Jesus tells us that some people pretend to have good fruit, but, "By their fruit you will recognize them. Do people pick grapes from thornbushes, or figs from thistles? Likewise every good tree bears good fruit, but a bad tree bears bad fruit. A good tree cannot bear bad fruit, and a bad tree cannot bear good fruit. Every tree that does not bear good fruit is cut down and thrown into the fire. Thus, by their fruit you will recognize them" (Matthew 7:16). Jesus concludes His 'Sermon on the Mount' with the call to follow Him and build our house on Him. In the next line He says, "Not everyone who says to me, 'Lord, Lord,' will enter the kingdom of heaven, but only he who does the will of my Father who is in heaven" (Matthew 7:21). With so much just from fruit, we begin to see how life-giving Jesus really is.[188]

Gelato al Cioccolato

Pictured is actually, 'Gelato *Espresso* con Cioccolato.' This last summer my brother, Nick Woods, and his girlfriend, Maria Enomoto, churned it *fatta in cassa* (Italian for *made at home*). Nick, who is currently studying neuroscience, and loves any science project, has recently taken to learning the art of coffee roasting. I have observed that this is quite an exact process as he measures by the ounce, considers the degree of coloring, and calculates the timing of the cracks. As for the ice cream making, I think we all realized that it is a real labor of love. The whole event took consistent churning, and at about every half hour for eight hours, Nick and Maria mixed it over ice in the bowl seen at the back of the photo. It was a wholesome experiment and they truly worked off the calories. (Also, an old, German burr coffee grinder is pictured at the back right!)

Since then, I have tried to make, 'Gelato al Cioccolato,' in an *ice-cream maker* (I love the espresso's taste, but refrained from using the beans because all coffees do raise your blood pressure). The modern process with the machine did involve some timely preparation, but turned out to be *a lot* easier! Regardless, in making the gelato, I found that it's quite the special treat. I reduced the fat and salt content as much as I could, but the dessert does require milk and cream for a reason. After these experiments, I'd say, it is important to sometimes celebrate with projects that take a little longer, and to use the finest ingredients you have in them, of course, *all for the LORD!*

In the Old Testament, especially in Leviticus, Exodus and Numbers, there are many accounts of people worshiping God with the finest things they have. It is healthy to note that all the senses are involved, because sometimes we think that worshiping God can only be through singing. Singing is an amazing form of worship, as seen throughout Scripture (especially in the Psalms), but God would probably love for us to learn more about Him and come closer to Him through other methods too! That is a reason to worship: to become closer to Him! For, He doesn't need worship Himself, but worship should be a fun expression of thanks for the glorious riches that He has bestowed on us. The greatest of these being life, accomplished through His Son's sacrifice and victory on the cross! Hallelujah! In Exodus, the LORD God gave regulations to Moses on all types of worship. Some of these included: how to make the ark, which held the Ten Commandments; some were for the finely selected incense; some were for the special and delicious meals to eat. God wants each sense to be involved to show that He alone is Holy and Worthy, and that He makes things for our good and enjoyment! Consider the regulations for the priestly . . . (See footnote 89 for the rest!)

Jesus' Word

Dessert as Bread of Life

Now, here is the best for last. As it is written, "But many who are first will be last, and many who are last will be first" (Matthew 19:30). Jesus showed that certain things we place low value on are actually the things to be valued the most. That is why this recipe is last, because it should actually be valued the most. God's Word to us is Jesus. God humbled Himself and became the Word in the flesh. John records, "In the beginning was the Word, and the Word was with God, and the Word was God. He was with God in the beginning" (John 1:1-2). John continues later with, "The Word became flesh and made his dwelling among us. We have seen his glory, the glory of the One and Only, who came from the Father, full of grace and truth" (John 1:14). Jesus is this Word. That is why the Word in the Bible is so important. Many verses are what Jesus said, and, "All Scripture is God-breathed and is useful for teaching, rebuking, correcting and training in righteousness, so that the man of God may be thoroughly equipped for every good work" (2 Timothy 3:16-17). All mankind should read what God has for us in the Bible, "For the word of God is living and active. Sharper than any double-edged sword, it penetrates even to dividing soul and spirit, joints and marrow; it judges the thoughts and attitudes of the heart" (Hebrews 4:12).

Sometimes, though, we (myself included) forget to read the Word. This is like going throughout the day without food. The first recipe in this book reminds us, "Then Jesus declared, 'I am the bread of life. He who comes to me will never go hungry, and he who believes in me will never be thirsty,'" (John 6:35; see also 5:48 and 6:51). Jesus is our daily sustenance, and Jesus leads us and guides us through His Holy Spirit to daily seek Him and help others. This fits with the greatest commandment, and the second, like it. Matthew records, "Jesus replied: "'Love the Lord your God with all your heart and with all your soul and with all your mind.' This is the first and greatest commandment. And the second is like it: 'Love your neighbor as yourself.' All the Law and the Prophets hang on these two commandments" (Matthew 22:37-40). Let's pray when we sit down to read the Bible, that God sends us His Holy Spirit and leads us with what to read. He will answer this prayer and give us the food we need for the day.

Trying to read the Word, or listen to God, can be challenging for different reasons. Think about this picture. If you quickly walked towards the Scripture, you would run straight into the glass slider. Instead, pray in Jesus' Name that He leads you and you'll easily learn to avoid obstacles that you yourself would miss. He will lead you around the table and into His Presence. Amen Hallelujah!

Notes

When skimming over the 'Notes' section in books, it may seem hard to read or investigate the sources. However, if you are reading this now, be challenged and continue! Within the citations that follow, there are a variety of formats and tools to help you and others. Even if you investigate only a few sources, you can praise God for His kindness and creativity in making nature so elegant. And you may be enabled to love someone by telling them healthy information. Loving God and loving others is the most healthy, though. Jesus said of the commandments, "'The most important one,' answered Jesus, 'is this: 'Hear, O Israel, the Lord our God, the Lord is one. Love the Lord your God with all your heart and with all your soul and with all your mind and with all your strength.' The second is this: 'Love your neighbor as yourself.' There is no commandment greater than these'" (Mark 12:29-31). Jesus included, "with all your mind," quoting God when He spoke to Moses through the burning bush (Deuteronomy 6:4-5). It's best to love God with *all* that we are, not just our minds, but, when we do use our minds, let's use them wisely to serve Him. Even if they're not on the subjects listed here, all things God gives us to learn are vital to loving Him and others more! God Bless and have fun praising God in all that you do with all that you are!

1. "Sodium: How to tame your salt habit now." Nutrition and healthy eating. Ed. Roger W. Harms, Kenneth G. Berge, Phillip T. Hagen, Scott C. Litin, and Sheldon G. Sheps. Mayo Clinic, 3 Mar. 2011. google. Web. 30 Aug. 2011. <http://www.mayoclinic.com/health/sodium/NU00284/NSECTIONGROUP=2>.

2. Blaustein MP, Zhang J, Chen L, et al: How does salt retention raise blood pressure? Am J Physiol Regul Integr Comp Physiol 290:514-523, 2006 <http://ndt.oxfordjournals.org/content/23/9/2723.full>.

3. Weir, Matthew R. "Dietary Fructose and Elevated Levels of Blood Pressure." Journal of the American Society of Nephrology 21.9 12 Aug. (2010): 1416-18. Web. 12 Jan. 2012. <http://jasn.asnjournals.org/content/21/9/1416.full>.

4. "Water: How much should you drink every day?." Nutrition and healthy eating. Ed. Roger W. Harms, Kenneth G. Berge, Phillip T. Hagen, Scott C. Litin, and Sheldon G. Sheps. Mayo Clinic, 17 Apr. 2010. google. Web. 30 Aug. 2011. <http://www.mayoclinic.com/health/water/NU00283>.

5. "Dietary fats: Know which types to choose." Nutrition and healthy eating. Ed. Roger W. Harms, Kenneth G. Berge, Phillip T. Hagen, Scott C. Litin, and Sheldon G. Sheps. Mayo Clinic, Feb. 2011. google. Web. 30 Aug. 2011. <http://www.mayoclinic.com/health/fat/NU00262>.

6. Adopted from Miller II, Damon P. "Omega 3-Omega 6 Ratios of Common Oils." Organic MD. N.p., n.d. Web. 20 Aug. 2011. <http://organicmd.com/omega-3-omega-6-ratios-of-common-oils/>.

7. AP, Simopoulos. "The importance of the ratio of omega-6/omega-3 essential fatty acids." PubMed.gov. PubMed, Oct. 2002. google. Web. 30 Aug. 2011. <http://www.ncbi.nlm.nih.gov/pubmed/ 12442909>.

8. Fletton, Helen. Wheat-Free.org. N.p., n.d. google. Web. 2 Sept. 2011. <http://www.wheat-free.org/wheat-free-flour.html>.

9. Raven, Peter H., George B. Johnson, Jonathan B. Losos, and Susan R. Singer. Biology, Seventh Edition. 7th ed. New York, NY: McGraw-Hill, 2005. ch.9 and 284, respectively. Print.

10. Lustig, Robert H., narr. Sugar: The Bitter Truth. You Tube, 2009. Web. 2 Sept. 2011. <http://www.youtube.com/watch?v=dBnniua6-oM>.

11. Raven, Peter H., George B. Johnson, Jonathan B. Losos, and Susan R. Singer. Biology, Seventh Edition. 7th ed. New York: McGraw-Hill, 2005. 120-22. Print.

12. Tajkhorshid, Emad, Klaus Schulten, Yi Wang, Jin Yu, and Fangqiang Zhu. "Structure, Dynamics, and Function of Aquaporins." Theoretical and Computational Biophysics Group. University of Illinois at Urbana-Champaign, 15 Oct. 2006. google. Web. 2 Sept. 2011. <http://www.ks.uiuc.edu/Research/aquaporins/>.

13. "Protein." Nutrition for Everyone. Centers for Disease Control and Prevention, n.d. google. Web. 2 Sept. 2011. <http://www.cdc.gov/nutrition/everyone/basics/protein.html>.

14. "Get Enough Protein In Vegetarian or Vegan Diets." Savvy Vegetarian. Savvy Vegetarian, n.d. google. Web. 2 Sept. 2011. <http://www.savvyvegetarian.com/articles/get-enough-protein-veg-diet.php>.

15. SELFNutritionData: know what you eat. Nutrition Data, n.d. google. Web. 2 Sept. 2011. <http://nutritiondata.self.com/>.

16. Lavelle, Peter. "Is Teflon safe?." The Pulse. ABC Health and Wellbeing, 23 Feb. 2006. google. Web. 3 Sept. 2011. <http://www.abc.net.au/health/thepulse/stories/2006/02/23/1576391.htm>.

17. Saftey of Teflon® non-sticks. DuPontTeflon®, n.d. google. Web. 3 Sept. 2011. <http://www2.dupont.com/Teflon/en_US/products/safety/index.html>.

Notes

18. Biello, David. "Plastic (Not) Fantastic: Food Containers Leach a Potentially Harmful Chemical." Scientific American. Scientific American, 19 Feb. 2008. google. Web. 3 Sept. 2011. <http://www.scientificamerican.com/article.cfm?id=plastic-not-fantastic-with-bisphenol-a>.

19. "Public Health Statement for Di(2-ethylhexyl)phtalate (DEHP)." Toxic Substances Portal - Di(2-ethylhexyl)phtalate (DEHP). ATSDR, Sept. 2002. Web. 3 Sept. 2011. <http://www.atsdr.cdc.gov/PHS/PHS.asp?id=376&tid=65>.

20. "Cast Iron Cookware - Cast iron Pans - Cast Iron Skillets." The Irreplaceable Cast Iron Pans. What's Cooking America, n.d. google. Web. 3 Sept. 2011. <http://whatscookingamerica.net/Information/CastIronPans.htm>.

21. White, Josh, narr. "A Worshiping Church." The Living Church. Door of Hope, under God's direction, Portland, 22 Aug. 2011. Web. 3 Sept. 2011. <http://www.doorofhopepdx.org/media/teachings/category/church-matters.html>.

22. Aletha, Aunt, and Dear O. Dave. "Cooking Terms Dictionary." New Italian Recipes. N.p., n.d. google. Web. 10 Sept. 2011. <http://www.newitalianrecipes.com/cooking-terms.html>.

23. Varieties of cherry tomatoes include: "Sungold, Camp Joy, Reisentraube, Chadwick's Cherry, Yellow Pear, Red Pear, Black Cherry, Blondkopfchen, and Green Grape" as listed by: "Cherry Tomato Varieties." Veggie Gardening Tips. N.p., 10 Apr. 2007. google. Web. 10 Sept. 2011. <http://www.veggiegardeningtips.com/cherry-tomato-varieties/>.

24. Besides plating in general, Ben has also developed 'snack-plating,' in which he lays out small proportions of seemingly non-realted foods. One time he had a hard-boiled egg with paprika, green beans, meats, orange slices and humus. Let's listen to Jesus and have fun getting our new food invention plated!

25. "Definition: hummus." Webster's Online Dictionary with Multilingual Thesaurus Translation. Ed. Phillip M. Parker. Webster's Dictionary Online, n.d. google. Web. 15 Sept. 2011. <http://www.websters-dictionary-online.com/definitions/hummus?cx=partner-pub-0939450753529744%3Av0qd01-tdlq&cof=FORID%3A9&ie=UTF-8&q=hummus&sa=Search#906>.

26. See hummus and humble, respectively:
Harper, Douglas. Online Etymology Dictionary. Douglas Harper, n.d. Web. 15 Sept. 2011. <http://www.etymonline.com/index.php?l=h&p=30>.

27. Pakhare, Jayashree. "Bruschetta." Buzzle.com: Intelligent Life on the Web. Buzzle.com, n.d. google. Web. 16 Sept. 2011. <http://www.buzzle.com/articles/bruschetta.html>.

28. White, Josh, narr. "Why Should We Sing?." Spirit and Truth. Door of Hope, under God's direction, Portland, 2011. Web. 21 Sept. 2011.
<http://www.doorofhopepdx.org/media/teachings/category/spirit-and-truth.html>.

29. White, Josh, narr. "What Is Worship?." Spirit and Truth. Door of Hope, under God's direction, Portland, 16 Aug. 2011. Web. 21 Sept. 2011.
<http://www.doorofhopepdx.org/media/teachings/category/spirit-and-truth.html>.

30. This is a perfect opportunity to explain how Sabrina's wonderful salad calls for canned black beans, black olives and canned broth. However, these ingredients should generally be avoided in a low-sodium diet (also, most canned foods are high in sodium). It is easy, though, to use alternatives. Soaking beans overnight in twice the amount of water, or by making your own broth as described in footnote 40, is cost efficient, fun and healthy! Praise God!

31. Sabrina mentioned, "You can add most any fresh vegetable: carrot, celery, cucumber, radish, cubed cooked squash . . . really anything to please your taste." I actually had a lot of left over sprouts that went well with her already great salad. Let's go for it and be inventive with His Holy Spirit leading the Way!

32. "The Christian Fish Symbol." Religion Facts. N.p., n.d. google. Web. 23 Sept. 2011.
<http://www.religionfacts.com/christianity/symbols/fish.htm>.
    Plus, Jesus said, "Do not think that I have come to abolish the Law or the Prophets; I have not come to abolish them but to fulfil them" (Matthew 5:17). Also, it is recorded in James that, "Religion that God our Father accepts as pure and faultless is this: to look after orphans and widows in their distress and to keep oneself from being polluted by the world" (James 1:27). Christianity is centred on Christ and what He has done in love, rather than on just rules, or a religion. For example, remember what Jesus said the greatest commandment was (recorded by the Gospel writers Matthew, Mark and Luke, it shows the importance. Jesus was quoting from Deuteronomy 6:4-5), "Jesus replied; 'Love the Lord your God with all your heart and with all your soul and with all your mind.' This is the first and greatest commandment. And the second is like it: 'Love your neighbor as yourself.' All the Law and the prophets hang on these two commandments" (Matthew 22:37-40). It is important to love first, and Jesus uses some basic rules to help us. That is why I think this site and other titles refer to 'religion.' But following religion does not save us . . .

only Jesus does, who lived a righteous life. He took our place on the cross, so that we don't have to, for the wages of sin is *death* (Romans 6:23). That is one reason why *life in Christ* is so awesome. Jesus is the Way, the Truth and the Life (John 14:6), and He is the only One who sets us free (Galatians 5:1)! Amen!

33. The two types of Salmon are Atlantic and Pacific (including Asian Pacific). *Atlantic* salmon is also its own species. It has many healthy fats and is thus more rich, but is sadly very over fished. The five species of Pacific Salmon include: Chinook (King, Tyee, Springer or Quannat), Sockeye (Redfish, Red, Blueback), Coho (Silver or Silverside), Chum (Dog or Calico), and Pink (Humpy or Humpback).[a] *Chinook* will taste more buttery, as many people mention, because of the higher fat and oil content. It would be better for the steamed preparation with bleu cheese as described on pg. 89.[b] *Sockeye* will give you that firm sesame seed or nutty flavor because of the salmon's diet in plankton. It would go great with this salad (pg. 47), or could be served more pure, recommended for sushi and other Asian dishes. *Coho* salmon is the mildest of the main three species, but would also be a great choice for this salad.[a] It is generally less expensive than the Chinook. *Chum* is even more mild, and most firm, but still offers many important oils with omega-3 fatty acids. *Pink* is not really recommended for culinary purposes, but is very helpful in reestablishing salmon populations.[b] An Asian Pacific salmon species is *Sakuramasu* (Cherry Salmon), but is mostly fished in Japan.[a] Speaking of this depletion in salmon, let us take care of the environment and preserve the gifts that God gives us from the sea. Consider how God had originally intended it, "Then God said, 'Let us make man in our image, in our likeness, and let them rule over the fish of the sea and the birds of the air, over the livestock, over all the earth, and over all the creatures that move along the ground'" (Genesis 1:26). If we deplete the resources, then we can't rule over them, or use them wisely. Also, consider how God said, "in our image." This is a reference to the Holy Trinity! (See also footnote 47.)

a. "Salmon Species: Know Your Salmon." Fine Salmon. N.p., n.d. google. Web. 24 Sept. 2011. <http://www.finesalmon.com/Salmon_Food/Salmon_Species/index.asp>.
b. Buchanan, David. "Salmon Varieties." Chef's Resources. Ed. David Buchanan. N.p., n.d. google. Web. 24 Sept. 2011. <http://www.chefs-resources.com/Fresh-Salmon-Varieties>.

34. To reiterate, shrimp have high amounts of protein per calorie, are low in saturated fat, offer a fine source of Iron, Zinc, Vitamin D, B12, and B3, and contain lots of omega-3 fatty acids. Additionally, shrimp are loaded with other minerals such as selenium, a major agent in antioxidants which helps to prevent cell deterioration and fights against cancer. The only apparent downfall may be shrimp's high cholesterol content, also a criticism of egg yellows. However, the amount of LDLs (bad cholesterol) in proportion to

HDLs (healthy cholesterol) after eating shrimp is decreased (whereas by eating whole eggs, the LDL levels are raised higher than the HDL's). Studies have also shown that triglyceride levels (bad fat) in the blood are decreased by about 13% after eating a diet with shrimp.[a] To learn more about eating healthy fats, and HDLs, read 'An Introduction to Oils and Fats,' pg. 10, and investigate the footnotes (4, 5, 6, 7) for that page and the one below. Plus, thank God for shrimp, huh!

a. "Shrimp." The World's Healthiest Foods. WHFoods, n.d. google. Web. 28 Sept. 2011. <http://www.whfoods.com/genpage.php?tname=foodspice&dbid=107>.

35. White, Josh, narr. "Why Simplicity?." The Four Pillars. Door of Hope, under God's direction, Portland, 26 Sept. 2011. Web. 26 Sept. 2011. <http://www.doorofhopepdx.org/media/teachings/category/the-four-pillars.html>.

36. "Peas, split, mature seeds, cooked, boiled, without salt." SELFNutritionData: know what you eat. Nutrition Data, n.d. google. Web. 1 Oct. 2011. <http://nutritiondata.self.com/facts/legumes-and-legume-products/4354/2>.

37. For the split pea soup, start by adding about 1 cup of water, or the leftover water that the peas were soaking in overnight. As you cook, the split peas will naturally reduce because of evaporation, leaving you with a heartier mixture. Continue adding enough water, stirring, and reducing until you reach your desired viscosity (thickness) and to prevent burning. I really like my split pea soup thick, so I do this process a few times. When re-serving the next day, use the same technique. Just pour in some water to heat up on the stove or in the microwave (use less water for the microwave).

Plus, if your looking for a way to serve others, that is awesome! Let's remember, though, it's not our service that saves us, but Jesus who saves us. He sacrificed His life for us on the cross! So, serving others through God's love and salvation shares His love with all His people! What a joy! If you would like a suggestion of how to serve, ask at your local church, or there are always ways to donate through ministries. A great one I have found is 'Samaritan's Purse.'[a] Additionally, anything that God gives you can be used to help others! Paul, the writer of Romans shares, "We have different gifts, according to the grace given us. If a man's gift is prophesying, let him use it in proportion to his faith. If it is serving, let him serve, if it is teaching, let him teach; if it is encouraging, let him encourage; if it is contributing to the needs of others, let him give generously; if it is leadership, let him govern diligently; if it is showing mercy, let him do it cheerfully" (Romans 12:6-8). Let's use the gifts God has specifically given us, out of His grace, to tell others about Him!

a. Samaritan's Purse. Samaritan's Purse, n.d. Web. 1 Oct. 2011. <http://www.samaritanspurse.org/>.

Notes

38. God used Moses in a special way. He thought of himself as too weak and not a strong speaker, but God spoke to him through a burning bush that was not consumed even though it burned. Then God continued to speak to all Israel through him and his brother, Aaron, who helped share what God said to Moses. (God could have spoken through Moses directly to the people, so God was displeased with his lack of obedience. However, God did give him help with his brother.) God will choose you to do amazing things through Him too, and not by your strength, but instead *with His strength*. All you have to do is trust! The next time God calls you, don't fear, for He will make you strong and carry out His good will.

   The story of Moses is recorded mainly in Exodus. And God called him through the burning bush in Exodus chapter 3. I would recommend reading this account because it is so amazing! Thank God for these, and also for His daily miracles of providing food, bread and life! (John 6:35, 48, 51)

39. The idea of Psalm 136 being read as a 'responsive reading' was adopted from the first Bible source listed below, the 'Life Application Bible.' This Bible has been an invaluable tool. It was given to me as a gift from Carol Steele, a true friend and sister in Christ.[a] It's also the Bible I've used for the verses in this book, in addition to 'Blue Letter Bible,' an online Bible resource.[b]

   a. Life Application Bible: New International Version. Wheaton And Grand Rapids: Tyndale House Publishers, Inc. and Zondervan, 1991. 1054-55, note 136: 1ff. Print.
   b. Blue Letter Bible. Blue Letter Bible, n.d. Web. 3 Oct. 2011. <http://www.blueletterbible.org/>.

40. To make the broth for a soup, quinoa, or something else, start at least a day in advance. (And for soups, soak any beans in twice the amount of water overnight. Depending upon which recipe you are following, use the cultural type of beans.) Begin then by boiling a 'stewing chicken' in about 15 liters of water, or at least enough water to completely cover the chicken. Place a metal stand at the bottom of the pot, such as a vegetable steamer, to prevent the chicken from burning. (If you don't use chicken, though, you can easily make the broth delicious without it. Just use about 7 liters of water to start.) Then add half of the vegetables and ingredients to the pot, such as: 1 long carrot, 1 1/2 celery stalks, 1/2 cup of white onion, lemon, basil, marjoram, Italian seasoning, a few bay leaves, fresh black pepper, other spices, and olive oil. You will save the other half for the following day. Next, boil over high heat for three hours, until the chicken is literally coming off the bone. Afterwards, remove the chicken from the broth, let it cool to the touch, then de-bone completely. Place in the refrigerator and return to the broth.

   Let the still hot broth cool for a while longer, about 20 minutes, and meanwhile stop-up your sink. Fill with cold water. Place the *whole* pot into the sink and let it cool for another 10 minutes. Now it's more prepared to set in the refrigerator (this process ensures that it is not at boiling temperature when entering your refrigerator, and not sitting out too long at room temperature). Say good night and look forward to tomorrow's harvest! God Bless your sleep.

The next day, you have your chicken, stock, and beans ready to go! While praising God, enjoy cooking. First, get the beans boiling. Take the beans out of their soaking water and boil in twice the amount of new water. They will take about 1 hour. During this time, remove your stock from the fridge. The stock has cooled, causing the fat to congeal and rise to the top. Skim the fat off the top, unless you really like it there, and begin to boil over high heat. (Now, this is as far as you'll need to go if your making quinoa, pg. 45!) For soups, continue by adding enough water to get the volume up to 15 liters again, along with the rest of the carrots, celery, and anything else that takes longer to soften. Then start to specialize! Read the three soup recipes for what to do, as they all differ slightly in cooking order, and timing. In general, add 1/4 of the remaining ingredients at the beginning and save the rest until the end or to use as a garnish. These three recipes change the soup dramatically, giving you a wide range of variety, yet, they still all share this similar start. This is similar to God in our lives. God is the constant, but He works through all our lives in so many amazing and unique ways. Remember, in everything, *His love endures forever*.

The soups taste great the first day (second day of preparation), but especially after resting in the fridge until the third total day. By waiting, the flavors have married and taste even better. This reminds me of how the LORD rose on the third day! Matthew records how Mary came on the third day to the tomb where Jesus was placed after His death on the cross. She saw an angel who said, "'Do not be afraid, for I know that you are looking for Jesus, who was crucified. He is not here; he has risen, just as he said. Come and see the place where he lay. Then go quickly and tell his disciples; 'He has risen from the dead and is going ahead of you into Galilee. There you will see him.' Now I have told you'" (Matthew 28:5-7). Jesus has risen indeed and is alive! Remember, *His love endures forever!*

41. See *minestrone* and *minister*, respectively:
Harper, Douglas. Online Etymology Dictionary. Douglas Harper, n.d. Web. 4 Oct. 2011.
<http://www.etymonline.com/index.php?l=h&p=30>.

42. If you serve others that is great! That is what God wants you to do. However, He wants you to do it with Him! Romans describes how we should be in Christ: "Therefore, there is now no condemnation for those who are in Christ Jesus," (Romans 8:1). If we are serving by ourselves, then it will make us tired and we won't be filled with God's love. Instead, let God work through you and it will be a joy to serve others!

Notes

43. Pine nuts contain high amounts of protein and manganese.[a] Eating the correct amount of manganese in our diets helps with bone formation, calcium absorption, and blood sugar regulation (manganese is also found in other nuts, as well as seeds, fruits and vegetables).[b] Plus, pine nuts are rich in antioxidants and have many other healthy benefits for us too![c] Thank God for His trees and His daily provision!

   a. "Nuts, pine nuts, dried." SELFNutritionData: know what you eat. SELFNutritionData, n.d. Web. 26 Oct. 2011. <http://nutritiondata.self.com/facts/nut-and-seed-products/3133/2>.
   b. "The Many Benefits of Manganese." Nutritional Supplements Health Guide. Nutritional Supplements Health Guide, n.d. google. Web. 26 Oct. 2011. <http://www.nutritional-supplements-health-guide.com/benefits-of-manganese.html>.
   c. "Pine nuts nutrition facts." Power your diet. Nutrition-and-you, n.d. google. Web. 26 Oct. 2011. <http://www.nutrition-and-you.com/pine-nuts.html>.

44. This is from Psalm 103:12. Psalm 103:11 goes with it as well. Together they read, "For as high as the heavens are above the earth, so great is his love for those who fear him; as far as the east is from the west, so far has he removed our transgressions from us."

45. The point of our relationship with Jesus is love; love from Him for He is real Love (1 John 4:8). Therefore, it is good to follow Christ's teachings because they help us see Him and set us free, but the reason for them should be *Him*! It's not based on us. He saves us! (See also footnotes 32, 56 and 63.) It is like a marriage. The point of a marriage should be love, *and actually love in Christ*, and out of joy, the married couple submits to one another. In fact, it was out of joy set before Him that Jesus has sacrificed Himself for us, i.e., the Church, i.e., *His bride* (Hebrews 12:1-29; Ephesians 5:29-33)! Now, because of *His sacrifice*, we can be with Him forever! This is not our work but His! So, there is no need to worry when we are with Him and doing what He teaches! Jesus has torn down all barriers between us and God forever (Matthew 27:51; Mark 15:38, and Luke 23:45), and offers *complete forgiveness to those who follow Him*! (These passages in the Gospels Matthew, Mark, and Luke describe how, when Jesus died, the curtain in the temple was torn from the top to bottom. This was yet another miracle by God and shows how *He* was taking down the spiritual separation between His people from Him. It used to be that only the high priest could go into the 'Most Holy place' behind the curtain once a year to make sacrifices for all the people. Since then, Jesus has become our 'Great High Priest' (Hebrews 5:7-10) and the Holy Spirit is sent to all of us so we can all know, hear, be with, and be in love with God all the time (John 15:26; footnote 47)!) We can really take heart that all our sins are forgiven, as far as the east is from the

west, when we abide in Him (Psalm 103:12)! He has done all these amazing miracles and more and truly loves us! Let's love Him back by *trusting in Him*. Let's also love others and reflect His love on them!

46. "The History of Pizza." Recipe Pizza: The worlds favorite Pizza recipe website. Recipe Pizza, n.d. google. Web. 7 Oct. 2011. <http://www.recipepizza.com/history_of_pizza.htm>.

47. God's Name is Holy, which means *set apart* or *devoted*, and God's Name is also like saying *His Character*.[ta] As was common practice in the Old Testament times, to name someone was to tell their relation to God; their character *in Him*. And all over the Bible, we can see that God's Character is: Holy and Righteous, Awesome and Beautiful, Admirable, Strong, the Best! This is why I say to "remember" God's Name, because it really could mean to think of Him, and how good He is (and He alone is good: Matthew 19:17). More specifically though, God's Name is given to Moses in Exodus 3:13-14. It is recorded, "Moses said to God, 'Suppose I go to the Israelites and say to them, 'The God of your father has sent me to you,' and they ask me, 'What is his name?' Then what shall I tell them?' God said to Moses, "I AM WHO I AM. This is what you are to say to the Israelites: I AM has sent me to you.'" This can also be translated to, "I WILL BE WHAT I WILL BE" and actually, "The Hebrew for LORD sounds like and may be derived from the Hebrew for I AM."[tb] God is telling Moses many things in His Name, but one idea that we get from it is that it is definitely Holy, Everlasting, Over all, Exalted, Final, Strong, and Full! In Exodus 3:15, it is also recorded that, "God also said to Moses, 'Say to the Israelites, 'The LORD, the God of your fathers - the God of Abraham, Isaac and Jacob - has sent me to you.' This is my name forever, the name by which I am to be remembered from generation to generation.'" God was sharing that He was the same God the previous generations had known. God is always here for us, desiring us to recognize Him, and yearning for us to be with Him! (Plus, the reason people capitalize His Name is to show His Holiness in text; to give Him credit because He deserves it! That is why I capitalize His Name in all the places I can.) Praise Him!

God also sent His only begotten Son, Jesus, who is fully God and fully human (Jesus means *the LORD saves*)![tc] His Name is given by God, revealed through an angel sent by God to Joseph, Mary's husband (as recorded in Matthew 1:20-21). Jesus is the Christ, or Messiah, which means *the Anointed One*.[td] Many people were awaiting a Messiah to come in the form of a military leader to save them from *Rome*, and Jesus came and offered salvation, but was different than what they had expected. He is a gentle leader who fought against spiritual evils, instead of against people. He came to *save* His people. The birth of Jesus fulfilled this specific prophecy (the prediction about a Savior) completely,

Notes

though. The prophecy said, "The virgin will be with child and will give birth to a son, and they will call him Immanuel' - which means, 'God with us'" (Matthew 1:23). So Jesus, or God, is also called Immanuel. (Isn't that cool too how Jesus' birth was predicted!) Plus, many other 'nick-names' are given to Jesus, such as: Wonderful Counselor, Mighty God, Prince of Peace, Alpha and Omega, Everlasting Father, Heavenly Father and Savior. All of these point again to how He loves and is Awesome in Character. Jesus continues in Revelation, "I am the Alpha and Omega, the First and the Last, the Beginning and the End" (Revelation 22:13), and, "I Jesus, have sent my angel to give you this testimony for the churches. I am the Root and the Offspring of David, and the bright Morning Star" (Revelation 22:16). Jesus teaches us it is important to remember His Name and know Him, for evil people will impersonate Him, but there is only One Jesus. Jesus warns, "'Watch out that no one deceives you. For many will come in my name, claiming, 'I am the Christ, and will deceive many'" (Matthew 24:4-5).† See, He kindly warns us ahead of time!

Additionally, the Holy Spirit is a part of God. Jesus said that He would leave for a while, but send the Holy Spirit. He said, "When the Counselor comes, whom I will send to you from the Father, the Spirit of truth who goes out from the Father, he will testify about me. And you must also testify, for you have been with me from the beginning" (John 15:26). Jesus rose to the Father, and now the Holy Spirit can be with all of us. Thus, we can be *with God all the time and anywhere!* This is such an overlooked gift! God gives us direct access to Him, His Holy Spirit, and we can pray - which essentially means talk - with Him always. And, "In the same way, the Spirit helps us in our weakness. We do not know what we ought to pray for, but the Spirit himself intercedes for us with groans that words cannot express" (Romans 8:26). God is directly available to us! Let's talk, and more importantly, *listen* to Him! It's a two way conversation.

The Name for God includes: God, Jesus, and the Holy Spirit. God exists in this Holy Trinity, which means that He is One God, yet has three separate parts at the same time. There is really no way to explain this other than that God is Awesome and above us. It is *not* a concept made up by theologians, though.†ᵉ Jesus Himself said, "Therefore go and make disciples of all nations, baptizing them in the name of the Father and of the Son and of the Holy Spirit, and teaching them to obey everything I have commanded you. And surely I am with you always, to the very end of the age" (Matthew 28:19-20). Jesus referred to the Name as singular. There is One God, as defined many times in the Bible (for example, see also Luke 3:21-22; John 1:29-34, and Genesis 1:26), and Jesus says that this Name is the Father, the Son, and the Holy Spirit: Three-In-One. There is no way to sit down and explain the Trinity, but I'm also glad that God is above my understanding because then I know He is above me!

God's Name essentially shows that He is God!

†There is more to Jesus' message on the end times, right before heaven. Look at least to Mt 24:1-25:46; Da 9:27, 11:31 and 12:11; Lk 21:7-38; 2Th 2:1-17; 1Jn, and Rev to start. Reading these is really important and shows that He is coming! This is awesome, but will also bring a lot of pain for those who want to reject Him. Jesus teaches many things about the end times such as how all of His followers - or people who love Him - will not be deceived, but that the others will be. We can recognize when Jesus comes back, though, because it will be extremely evident. And *He is telling us about it*; no one will need to tell us. Thus the phrases, "Where there is a dead body, there the vultures will gather" (Luke 17:37), and, "For as lightning that comes from the east is visible even in the west, so will be the coming of the Son of Man" (Matthew 24:27). Jesus is just being honest about all of this. He plainly explains, "See, I have told you ahead of time" (Matthew 24:25). Jesus wants to tell us these warnings and give us *opportunity* to be with Him and receive His love! It is also mentioned in Daniel, which you should read, that there will be an end to the daily sacrifice and an evil ruler will come to set up his own image to be worshiped instead. However, after this brief time, Jesus is victorious forever! From that point, the abolishing of the daily sacrifice and setting up the abomination that causes desolation, there will be 1290 days. In Daniel it says, "Blessed is the one who waits for and reaches the end of the 1335 days" (Daniel 12:12). Jesus and His return will be unmistakable for those who know Him, and for those He knows (Matthew 7:21-29). Let's be with Jesus! (See also footnote 78.)

a. See the 'Holiness' explanation in the Introduction to Leviticus, pg. 169

b. See footnotes f and g, respectively, pg. 109

c. See footnote c, pg. 1641

d. See footnote b, pg. 1640

e. See footnote n, pg. 1721, and the notes on the bottom of the page for verses 18, 18-20, 19, 19, 20 and 20, pg. 1721

Life Application Bible: New International Version. Wheaton And Grand Rapids: Tyndale House Publishers, Inc. and Zondervan, 1991. 169, 109, 1641, 1640 and 1721, respectively. Print.

48. I can almost taste this salad and recall the feeling of the Sabbath when I write about them! I hope you enjoy both in Him! For making the chicken, with any salad or dish, consider what it is complimenting. With this specific plate (*piatti* in Italian) the flavors are lighter and sweeter. Thus, the chicken is seasoned to be less pronounced and more lemony. It puts the other ingredients first. You can apply the complimentary strategy to additional meat preparations, vegetables, and also the people you are with. Compliment their strengths and interests. In 1 Corinthians 9:19-27, Paul writes, "Though I am free and belong to no man, I make myself a slave to everyone, to win as many as possible. To the Jews I became like a Jew, to win the Jews. To those under the law I became like one under the law (though I myself am not under the law), so as to win those under the law. To those not having the law I became like one not

having the law (though I am not free from God's law but am under Christ's law), so as to win those not having the law. To the weak I became weak, to win the weak. I have become all things to all men so that by all possible means I might save some. I do all this for the sake of the gospel, that I may share in its blessings. Do you not know that in a race all the runners run, but only one gets the prize? Run in such a way as to get the prize. Everyone who competes in the games goes into strict training. They do it to get a crown that will not last; but we do it to get a crown that will last forever. Therefore I do not run like a man running aimlessly; I do not fight like a man beating the air. No, I beat my body and make it my slave so that after I have preached to others, I myself will not be disqualified for the prize."
Amen and Hallelujah! (See also, 'Steak and Vegetable Shish Kebabs,' pg. 111!)

49. Philippians is a letter that Paul, an apostle of Christ Jesus, wrote to the Church in Philippi (*apostle* is from the Greek word, *apóstolos*, meaning *one who is sent out*[a]). These verses are so amazing and give some insight into Christ's attitude, especially in the face of adversity. If you are facing hard times, consider God, who has gone before you (Hebrews 6:19-20), who is providing just enough for you (Matthew 6:11; Luke 11:3; Exodus 16:14-36), and who completely understands your spot more than any other because He is not only with you right now, through the Holy Spirit (John 16:7), but He suffered death on a cross for you (Hebrews 12:1-29)! He knew that the temporary pain would bring about good in God! Here is the complete section of verses from Philippians 2:1-11. You can continue reading more after verse 11, but this is a start. Paul writes, "If you have any encouragement from being united with Christ, if any comfort from his love, if any fellowship with the Spirit, if any tenderness and compassion, then make my joy complete by being like-minded, having the same love; being one in spirit and purpose. Do nothing out of selfish ambition or vain conceit, but in humility consider others better than yourselves. Each of you should look not only to your own interests, but also to the interests of others. Your attitude should be the same as that of Christ Jesus: Who being in very nature God, did not consider equality with God something to be grasped, but made himself nothing, taking the very nature of a servant, being made in human likeness. And being found in appearance as a man, he humbled himself and became obedient to death - even death on a cross! Therefore God exalted him to the highest place and gave him the name that is above every name, that at the name of Jesus every knee should bow, in heaven and on earth and under the earth, and every tongue confess that Jesus Christ is Lord, to the glory of God the Father."

a. "Apostle." Origin. Dictionary.com. 2011. N. pag. Web. 19 Oct. 2011.
<http://dictionary.reference.com/browse/apostle>.

50. Serve the salmon a little under-cooked (just a bit!) as it will continue cooking on the plate. (This is also true with steak, which becomes more juicy if it is slightly under-cooked, covered with foil, and then served about 7 minutes later.) Additionally, try cooking the salmon in different ways. An alternate method that accentuates the nuttier and sweeter salmon tastes, preferably with Sockeye, is described on pg. 47 (read footnote 33 for salmon species and flavors). The steamed preparation that we did for my mom's birthday goes really well with the buttery Chinook and I, for one, love the bleu cheese. However, consider your guests!

    When plating, take the salmon off the skins. You can easily slide a spatula in-between at this time, as the salmon is very moist. The skin that is stuck to the pan can be soaked in warm water and then removed later. If it is hard to remove, read more on 'Pan Care,' pg. 21. Try pouring some water into the pan, then set to high heat, cover, and let steam for about 7 minutes. Gently clean the cast iron with a wooden spatula and return to the sink to rub with a dish towel (if using a stainless steel pan, you can vigorously clean with a metal spatula, sponge or mineral wool. These, and soap, however, would remove the cast iron's surface). Enjoy serving others in Christ first, and through Christ first, with these tips (Mt 25:31-46)!

51. The record of the people at the shrimp pizza dinners may seem a bit strange! It is modelled after the Old Testament way of recording people. At that time, record keeping like this was a method to reveal something had actually occurred, by pointing to the people there as witnesses, and to establish genealogies; it showed that ancestors were still being led by and cared for by God. So, the listing may seem odd, but it has great merit. Consider the genealogy of Jesus as recorded in Matthew 1:1-17. Let's start with this verse about Jesus. It reads, "and Jacob the father of Joseph, the husband of Mary, of whom was born Jesus, who is called Christ" (Matthew 1:16). Matthew 1 is usually glanced over, but I heard a pastor once note, "There is so much here!" The interesting people, all with stories connecting to God, culminate in the birth of Christ who is God's only begotten Son! He is our Savior! Thank Jesus for all His people and that they can point to Him! Let's remember these characters here, and in other genealogies, to learn more about Him and His love. For example, just look to verse five which includes Rahab. Rahab's story is recorded mostly in Joshua 2 and 6, but she is also mentioned in Hebrews 11:31 as a woman of great faith. She was a character society would have rejected, but because of her faith in Christ, she was redeemed in His sight! There are many other beautiful stories of people who trusted in the LORD, and they all point to how God is always merciful and just! Plus, God's story in our lives involves *everybody*. Jesus' genealogy includes all different walks of life. Since God loved us all first

Notes

through Jesus, let's respond with faith to love Him and all others back! For, when we receive His love in us (which is awesome), then He can be clearly shared with all! Hallelujah!

Secondly, you'll note that there are sometimes notes to the genealogies (the comments in Matthew 1: 6, 11, 12, and 16), like my parentheses in the pizza example. These extra descriptions show that the writers were trying to be as accurate as possible. The events and genealogies really happened! Biblical writers aimed to be accurate to relay the fullness of the miracles going on, so that everyone could hear about Jesus and not miss anything about His amazing truth! He does love us and He did come to save us! Let's follow after Him and do as He says, *because He is Truth*! (John 2:5 and John 14:6, respectively)

And finally, genealogies show how *God's Word to us* is always true and reliable! In this genealogy of Jesus Christ, recorded in Matthew, the reader can understand that God is faithful through His fulfilment of prophecies. There are actually <u>many</u> prophecies about Jesus' birth and Him being a descendent of David, <u>all</u> of which are fulfilled (Hallelujah!). Some of these include (1) Isaiah 9:6-7; (2) Isaiah 10:33-11:1 where Judah, which is the royal line of David, would be like the trees cut down, but then the Messiah, Jesus, would rise as a shoot from the stump; (3) Jeremiah 23:5-7; (4) 2 Samuel 7:11-16 about Jesus coming to be the LORD Himself who, "will establish a house for you" (2 Samuel 7:11), and (5) Acts 2:22-41! The prophecies all point to Jesus being the Messiah (Hebrew for "*the Anointed One*") coming to save everyone from their sins! I would recommend reading the above passages. Jesus' coming was truly predicted (also read in Matthew and footnotes 66b and 67)! The records really show these events happened and furthermore that Jesus is risen! What He offers is Truth. He gives us His Life! (John 14:6)

For a long time, I would often glance over the listings of people, or similar 'small' lessons in the Bible. Now, as I'm trying to read through the Old Testament, I'm finding so many connections and lessons about God's beauty when I actually slow down and read them out. God is real and He has given His Son to die on the cross for our sins! He has revealed Himself throughout His-story and is continuing to do so! His news of saving us, not by our works, but by His grace, is Good News indeed, and is shown true in every detail as recorded in all the Bible, guided by His Holy Spirit (2 Timothy 3:16-17)! God is amazing!

52. The double colander can be used to cook without direct or uneven heat. In this case, it keeps the dough warm, and not too hot, or else the yeast will denature and not work properly. To set it up, use two bowls per amount of dough. The inside bowl is smaller and contains the dough with some flour to prevent sticking. The outer bowl is filled half-way with warm water, and then the smaller bowl is placed inside. You can also set a towel and/ or hot pad on top to keep the yeast nice and cozy. Praise God that the culinary arts have met this scientific setup!

53. Bouillabaisse originated from a recipe that was need-based and inventive. It is fascinating how nowadays, this seafood masterpiece is such a special treat. The verses in Matthew 19:30 are when Jesus teaches, "but many who are first will be last, and many who are last will be first" (see also Mark 10:31). Jesus shows His kingdom values love and truth, not the outer 'success' that the world has to offer. Jesus also explains that loving Him and others is what matters most, rather than how we can get ahead (Matthew 22:37, Mark 12:30, and Luke 10:27 are quoted from Deuteronomy, mostly Deuteronomy 6:5). Interestingly, the heart of this seafood, the idea of all the flavors lovingly working together, is what has lasted, not the fads of the time. This reflects how His love does endure forever (Psalm 136)!

It is cool, too, how the seafood works together, and that in making this meal, my *family and I worked together* (we were also glad that we were at the Liggett's beach house. They are so kind to let us stay there)! Working together goes hand-in-hand with loving your neighbor as yourself and allows relationships to be made. Often times, the best things come out of relationships, and overcoming adversity. And actually, even 'by ourselves' we should still be working with God, so really all things are relationship-based! We can see that God is all about relationships. He wants to be in a relationship with us, He is Himself a relationship, as seen by the Holy Trinity relationship (see footnote 47), and He offers love to *us all* through His Son! Let's work together in Him by His love, grace and peace! Amen!

Louie Olivares, a pastor and friend, told me that bouillabaisse was based of the end of the day's catch. He also told me that Chileans have a similar recipe called *mariscada*, but that it had different origins. I really enjoyed hearing him share this His-story as well as how his mother would make the best mariscada and other interesting cuisines. I think it is remarkable that God has given us food - physically and spiritually (John 1:1-2, 14; 6:35, and pgs. 25 and 132). With His gift, we can see His creativity, and use it to interact with others. Also, His active love is daily shown to us by providing nice tasting, beautiful and sustaining options. Let's share in His love with Him by giving Him thanks, and share His love with others by donating food and spending time with them! God is so great!

54. red pepper. Sear for 5 minutes on high heat, then slightly reduce the temperature and cook for another 5 minutes adding pepper jack cheese at the end. The sweet and lightly charred taste from frying the salmon compliments the bouillabaisse quite well. (For more explanation of this type of salmon preparation, preferably with Sockeye, see pg. 47. For a rich and buttery steamed salmon, choose Chinook and see pg. 89. And for more information on salmon selection in general, see footnote 33.) When the salmon is finished, place with the clams or mussels in the double colander to keep warm (footnote 52). Then, begin the scallops. You can use the same pan that the clams or mussels were in to start off the seasoning right.

Notes

If desired, add 1 more Tbsp chopped green onion, 1 Tbsp basil, 3 garlic cloves, 1/2 lemon, olive oil, red pepper flakes, and black pepper to re-season the pan. Fry the scallops on high heat for 5-7 minutes until they become flaky, not rubbery. Set these in the double colander as well. Then start the prawns. You should always devein and de-shell, but whether or not you leave the tails on is your choice (and remember, to make them appear more gourmet, butterfly by scoring the back (pg. 86)). Place them in the same hot pan you've been using, and add: 1 Tbsp white wine, 1/4 lemon, olive oil, rosemary, marjoram, red pepper flakes, black pepper and a small amount of chili powder (some chili powder always goes well with shrimp)! Pan fry the shrimps for 7-10 minutes until pink and flaky, not rubbery, adding the garlic near the end. Set in the warm double colander and toss with some fresh basil just before adding to the broth.

While making the seafood, keep an eye on the broth that has been boiling for an hour. After the hour, add the crab legs. Then let these guys cook in there for another 30 minutes as you finish the rest of the seafood preparation.

After everything is set, and the 1 1/2 hours have passed, take all the seafood except for the salmon (you'll keep that out until the very end) and add to the broth. At this point also add a new set of ingredients: 1 more Tbsp green onion, 5-7 garlic cloves, 1/4 lemon, and the same dried spices as before, but in smaller quantities. Let the bouillabaisse combine over high heat for another 15 minutes. You'll probably be really eager to eat at this point, but it is just getting better with time!

You are about ready! Turn the heat down to a low simmer and gently add in the salmon with: 1 Tbsp cilantro, 1 Tbsp serrano pepper (this is not that spicy for all this bouillabaisse but feel free to increase or decrease this amount), 1/4 more lemon, 1/2 lime, and 1/2 cup red onion. I would also add 1/2 to 3/4 cup mozzarella cheese and some more red pepper and/ or black pepper to taste.

And finally . . . you're there!!! To serve the bouillabaisse to your friends or family, take some broth, the *fruits de mer*, and garnish it up. Add a few green thyme sprigs, fresh cilantro, chopped garlic and lemon or lime wedges! Also, try serving it with some pan-seared French garlic bread. Rub each side with olive oil and minced garlic, then sear on a pan at medium heat for 3-4 minutes. This will give you a nice soft-toasted bread. Traditionally, the bread was dipped into the broth first and the seafood was eaten second. What a wonderful treat! Praise the LORD! (I'll mention, too, that I have found by putting garlic in the whole pot at the end, the bouillabaisse, or any soup for that matter, can taste a bit odd. I'm not sure why yet, but the raw garlic takes on a different taste when steeped. Therefore, you should probably only add garlic in the beginning of the soup making process, and/ or as a personal garnish. This will ensure that the garlic cooks all the way and will not leave that strange taste in your pot!) I hope you enjoy the delicious bouillabaisse

(I'll miss writing that) and can focus on God and how He has graciously given you so many opportunities in Him; opportunities to work together with Him and others, to be creative in Him, and to grow in His plans of love for you. Remember that His plans for you are, "plans to prosper you and not to harm you, plans to give you a hope and a future" (Jeremiah 29:11). His plans might not be worldly 'riches,' or what the world values, but He offers an everlasting, glorious relationship with Him and His people dwelling in truth and true riches of love and peace forever. Hallelujah!

(Note that the picture at the Liggett's beach house has fresh bread because it was taken right before my brother, Nick, had pan-seared it!)

55. We love the Liggetts and their beach house! Seriously, thank you so much Liggetts for letting us stay there. We always feel Jesus' joy and peace in your home! It is one of our family's favorite places in the whole world. I cannot write enough about how blessed I have been to spend time with the LORD and our family there! Thanks so much and God Bless you all too!

56. Only with God's help, David was shepherd at one point, the David who defeated Goliath, later a king, the writer of many Psalms, and an ancestor of Jesus! He seems like a pretty cool guy. He made mistakes in his life though, like all of us do in heart or deed, and needed God for forgiveness to be in a righteous relationship. And, he relied on God for continual guidance and strength! Here, in Psalm 28, David is describing how he worshiped God and gave thanks through song. We also should worship God! It is really fun, amazing, and is a gift God gives to us for entering into a conversation with Him. Simply *being* with God is really the best gift, and is only made possible through Him, by the Holy Spirit (John 14:16, 26; 15:26, and 16:7 to start). So let's enjoy the gift He has given us *for Him!*

Worship though, should not be religious, or boring. For example, David suggested a song, but really anything we do can be done for God with a spirit of worship (look at pg. 41 or footnote 37 too)! Jesus said of some people, "They worship me in vain; their teachings are but rules taught by men" (Mark 7:7). Therefore, what Jesus really desires is our heart, soul, mind and strength to be with Him (Mark 12:30-31). It is like a husband and wife relationship, where their lives are invested in each other's. Jesus has already invested in us. He laid down His life for us because He loved us so much! "For God so loved the world that he gave his one and only Son, that whoever believes in him shall not perish but have eternal life. For God did not send his Son into the world to condemn the world, but to save the world through him" (John 3:16-17). God sent His only Son to die for our sins so we don't have to! Just by having faith in His work we now have eternal life in Jesus! Let's use anything that God has given us to

Notes

thank Him! Colossians 3:23-24 says, "Whatever you do, work at it with all your heart, as working for the Lord, not for men, since you know that you will receive an inheritance from the Lord as a reward. It is the Lord Christ you are serving." In everything we do, we get to thank God!

Jesus also talked about true worship in John 4:23-24. This contrasts worshiping in vain, and using rules taught by men. Jesus says instead, "Yet a time is coming and has now come when the true worshipers will worship the Father in spirit and truth, for they are the kind of worshipers the Father seeks. God is spirit, and his worshipers must worship in spirit and in truth" (John 4:23-24). God has given us so much including Jesus' sacrifice! Let's truly worship Him with every gift! (See also pgs. 41 and 131!)

57. "A holiday at the sea" is definitely what we had here, both literally and in time spent with God. This phrase is from C.S. Lewis', "The Weight of Glory," where Lewis is describing how some people are like young lads who are too preoccupied, or whatever, with their grime to look at what God has to offer. Lewis says, "Indeed, if we consider the unblushing promises of reward and the staggering nature of the rewards promised in the Gospels, it would seem that Our Lord finds our desires, not too strong, but too weak. We are half-hearted creatures, fooling about with drink and sex and ambition when infinite joy is offered us, like an ignorant child who wants to go on making mud pies in a slum because he cannot imagine what is meant by the offer of a holiday at the sea. We are far too easily pleased." The holiday at the sea is all of the joy and peace and freedom that we can experience in Christ, because that is really who He is. Those are some of His character traits! God is so awesome and worthy of praise and time spent with Him. Let's look to Him in everything! "Therefore, since we are surrounded by such a great cloud of witnesses, let us throw off everything that hinders and the sin that so easily entangles, and let us run with perseverance the race marked out for us. Let us fix our eyes on Jesus, the author and perfecter of our faith, who for the joy set before him, endured the cross, scorning its shame, and sat down at the right hand of the throne of God. Consider him who endured such opposition from sinful men, so that you will not grow weary and loose heart" (Hebrews 12:1-3).

58. "all the saints" refers to those who believe in Christ Jesus! We should ask for anything in His Name, but remember to have it for Him (John 14:14; James 4:3)! Praise God that He works miracles daily!

59. In Matthew 21:21, "Jesus replied, 'I tell you the truth, if you have faith and do not doubt, not only can you do what was done to the fig tree, but also you can say to this mountain, 'Go, throw yourself into the sea,' and it will be done.'" Jesus is showing that no miracle is too big. Anything we ask for in Jesus' Name

(James 4:3 tells about it being for Him, not us!) when we believe and do not doubt, will happen, even with a small amount of faith. Jesus is the one doing it, not us. Also, Jesus will reveal Himself to all people, as described in Revelation. All people will know *about* Him at some point, but not everyone will *know* Him. Jesus warned us about just knowing about Him, but not being in a relationship with Him. He said, "Not everyone who says to me, 'Lord, Lord,' will enter the kingdom of heaven, but only he who does the will of my Father who is in heaven. Many will say to me on that day, 'Lord, Lord, did we not prophesy in your name, and in your name drive out demons and perform many miracles?' Then I will tell them plainly, 'I never knew you. Away from me, you evildoers!' Therefore everyone who hears these words of mine and puts them into practice is like a wise man who built his house on a rock. The rain came down, the streams rose, and the winds blew and beat against that house; yet it did not fall, because it had its foundation on the rock. But everyone who hears these words of mine and does not put them into practice is like a foolish man who built his house on the sand. The rain came down, the streams rose, and the winds blew and beat against that house, and it fell with a great crash.' When Jesus had finished saying these things, the crowds were amazed at his teaching, because he taught as one who had authority, and not as their teachers of the law" (Matthew 7:21-29).

60. Kale Steak (The Bodega Special)

To start the 'Kale Steak,' first select your kale and asada. There are many types of kale (and chard) so try a variety! For the asada, visit your local bodega. You can get it pre-marinated or sometimes you'll just choose the cut. The marinades they offer are so delicious, but on occasion salty. Experiment with your own salt free version at home too. Marinate for an hour to a day with red onions, cilantro, garlic, lemon, lime, red pepper flakes, cayenne pepper, chili powder, serrano pepper, jalapeño pepper, and olive oil.

The next day, soften the kale and chard over a medium high heat, adding the onions, olive oil, onion powder and brown sugar. Then add the asada with spices, more brown sugar, and some garlic, lime and orange juice. Combine with the slivered almonds until they have goldened. Serve with lime wedges to garnish and recall His works He began in you! (Philippians 1:6)

4-7 leaves of kale

3-4 leaves of chard

1 lb asada (*marinated or try marinating it at home with no salt: see recipe*)

1/2 white onion, sliced

3-4 garlic cloves

1 Tbsp slivered, unsalted almonds

1/2 lime and a dash of orange juice

Red pepper, black pepper, onion powder, brown sugar and olive oil to taste

Notes

61. *Bodega* is a term I first heard from my dear lifelong friend, Jordan Johnson. As an avid Spanish speaker and learner of Spanish culture, he is always incorporating interesting words into our conversations. This word, he tells me, first referred to an industrial complex, or building with equipment in it. However, the English usage refers more to the 'corner market.' Jordan first heard this term from the Paul Simon song, "Diamonds on the Soles of Her Shoes." Jordan said tonight, "I love the way that line flows out. It's my favorite line of that song." I completely agree! And I just realized, let's pray that we use Scripture like this line, and also in our conversations! Whenever we hear something from God, let's share it with others so that they can hear His beauty as well! Hallelujah for God speaking to us through Jordan's interests!

62. 'Kale-Steak' was the first meal in which I really felt led by God to make the He Art cookbook. I thought, "Ok, God, this would be really cool, you're right!" I'm really thankful that God put this on my heart, that He helped me listen, and pray that His love can be made known to people through this book. And may anything we do be for Him (even cooking)! Colossians 3:17 says, "And whatever you do, whether in word or deed, do it all in the name of the Lord Jesus, giving thanks to God the Father through him." Whatever God has given to us, let us do it for Him! (Romans 12:8 gives some examples of working for God. I have used this verse several times, but it is so right. It is also quoted in footnote 37.)

    The verses in Matthew 25:31-46 describe the second part of doing all things for Him. We should do all things with Him working through us, and 'to' Him. Matthew 25:31-46 says, "When the Son of Man comes in his glory, and all the angels with him, he will sit on his throne in heavenly glory. All the nations will be gathered before him, and he will separate the people one from another as a shepherd separates the sheep from the goats. He will put the sheep on his right and the goats on his left. 'Then the King will say to those on his right, 'Come, you who are blessed by my Father; take your inheritance, the kingdom prepared for you since the creation of the world. For I was hungry and you gave me something to eat, I was thirsty and you gave me something to drink, I was a stranger and you invited me in, I needed clothes and you clothed me, I was sick and you looked after me, I was in prison and you came to visit me.' 'Then the righteous will answer him, 'Lord, when did we see you hungry and feed you, or thirsty and give you something to drink? When did we see you a stranger and invite you in, or needing clothes and clothe you? When did we see you sick or in prison and go to visit you?' 'The King will reply, 'I tell you the truth, whatever you did for one of the least of these brothers of mine, you did for me.' 'Then he will say to those on his left, 'Depart from me, you who are cursed, into the eternal fire prepared for the devil and his angels. For I was hungry and you gave me nothing to eat, I was thirsty and you gave me nothing to drink, I was a stranger and you did not invite me in, I needed clothes and you did not clothe me, I was sick and in prison and you did not look after me.' 'They also will answer, 'Lord, when did we see you hungry or thirsty or a stranger or needing clothes or sick or in prison, and did not help you?' 'He will reply, 'I tell you the truth, whatever you did not do for one of the least of these, you did not do for me.' 'Then they will go away to eternal punishment, but the righteous to eternal life.'" I have used this Scripture reference a few times as well, but it is also so right. Earlier this evening at Church, too, it was one of the prominent passages used throughout the sermon. I know God wanted at least for me to hear it and I'm joy-filled to share His Good News with you. Hallelujah! I know God desires for you to hear His message. I would encourage you to listen to this sermon. God Bless your listening!

Wilder, Josh, narr. "The Merciful" The Beatitudes. Door of Hope, under God's direction, Portland, 9 Nov. 2011. Web. 7 Nov. 2011. <http://www.doorofhopepdx.org/media/teachings/category/the-beatitudes.html>.

63. Chicken pot pie often contains chicken broth. You can add it to this recipe as well, but be cautious of the high salt content in store-bought varieties. Thank God, though, because making it at home is easy! For information on making your own salt free chicken broth, or vegetable broth, read footnote 40.

    The crust in pies is what usually contains most of the saturated fat. Butter and shortenings provide the elastic and textural qualities that we are used to. This recipe's crust is a bit different, but hopefully can be learned to be loved for the healthy benefits. Try experimenting with learning new methods to make recipes healthier, e.g., by using xanthan gum, which gives an elastic quality to gluten-free dishes.

    When thinking of how fat is used, I was reminded of how God often declared to the Israelites - His chosen people in the Old Testament times - that they should not eat the fat in offerings. Most of His instructions to them are recorded in Leviticus and Numbers. Leviticus is generally about how to worship God, and Numbers is about the census God had Moses take of the Israelites, and them moving through the desert to the Promised Land. Here is a verse about not eating the fat in Leviticus 7:22, "The Lord said to Moses, 'Say to the Israelites: 'Do not eat any of the fat of cattle, sheep or goats. The fat of an animal found dead or torn by wild animals may be used for any other purpose, but you must not eat it. Anyone who eats the fat of an animal from which an offering by fire may be made to the LORD must be cut off from his people." God had many other rules about offerings and worship, but they were all set out to help people. We can see how if people ate too much fat back then, or other animals such as oysters (a lot of the food regulations are in Leviticus 11), they would have probably become sick or died. This was God's protection for them. He was very serious about these regulations and also for sin, so obviously sin is also life-threatening. In fact, we read in Romans 6:23: "For the wages of sin is death, but the gift of God is eternal life in Christ Jesus our Lord." Thus, we can see the practices in Leviticus were practical back then, but still morally applicable to us today. Also, in the New Testament, we learn that Jesus came and fulfilled the Law. Jesus said, "Do not think that I have come to abolish the Law or the Prophets; I have not come to abolish them but to fulfil them. I tell you the truth, until heaven and earth disappear, not the smallest letter, not the least stroke of a pen, will by any means disappear from the Law until everything is accomplished" (Matthew 5:17-18). Jesus was showing that He is the way, not the rules, because religion had sadly become the false focus. Jesus is the way, the truth and the life and Who to focus on! John records, "Jesus answered, "I am the way and the truth and the life. No one comes to the Father except through me" (John 14:6). Praise God that He has provided the Way for us!

Jesus showed how many practices that were originally intended to help people had become harmful. Jesus told them that it was not really the food that they put into their mouths, but rather what they said, that could make them unclean. In His Words, He said, "Don't you see that whatever enters the mouth goes into the stomach and then out of the body? But the things that come out of the mouth come from the heart, and these make a man 'unclean.' For out of the heart come evil thoughts, murder, adultery, sexual immorality, theft, false testimony, slander. These are what make a man 'unclean'; but eating with unwashed hands does not make him 'unclean'" (Matthew 15:17-20). Matthew 12:34 also records Jesus talking to hypocrites about the heart. Jesus says, "You brood of vipers, how can you who are evil say anything good? For out of the overflow of the heart the mouth speaks." Jesus was breaking down ideas of men, and showing that His life and how He loved was what matters. By saying these things, He was also declaring that all foods were ceremonially clean. Today, we should still try to eat in moderation to stay healthy though. And fortunately, we have more research and culture to understand how to eat other foods, like seafoods, safely. But, Jesus' moral teachings still apply! Our hearts depend on Him and His sacrifice for us on the cross. He died for us, so that we don't have to! Let's remain in Him!

64. To transfer the dough to the pie pan's bottom, roll the dough out on top of some parchment paper covered with flour. Then, place the pie pan upside down over the dough, and turn the whole unit back over (you can also use a cookie sheet underneath). Gently work the dough into the corners of the pan.

To place the top on, use the parchment paper again. Roll out the dough over a floured piece and then pick it up in the middle, folding it in half, dough side out. Bring it over the pie and starting with one half, gently unfold or unroll it. Trim the excess and pinch, frill, or bind the sides in a nice way.

These instructions are easier said than done. It is also easier to say that we will help others than to actually do so. Let's start with our families and the people God has in our lives that are closest to us. These are the relationships that God has for us, to show people His love. Let's also *rely on His love and peace*, letting Him guide us so that it is not our burden. Matthew 11:28-30 says, "Come to me, all you who are weary and burdened, and I will give you rest. Take my yoke upon you and learn from me, for I am gentle and humble in heart, and you will find rest for your souls. For my yoke is easy and my burden is light."

Also, here are the last verses mentioned on this page from James 2:14-26. It is so important to really help people in Christ. Let's really do so! The verses read, "What good is it, my brothers, if a man claims to have faith but has no deeds? Can such faith save him? Suppose a brother or sister is without clothes and daily food. If one of you says to him, 'Go, I wish you well; keep warm and well fed,' but does nothing about his physical needs, what good is it? In the same way, faith by itself, if it is not accompanied by action, is dead. But someone will say, 'You have faith; I have deeds.' Show me your faith without deeds, and I will show you my faith by what I do. You believe that there is one God. Good! Even the demons believe that - and shudder. You foolish man, do you want evidence that faith without deeds is useless? Was not our ancestor Abraham considered righteous for what he did when he offered his son Isaac on the altar? You see that his faith and his actions were working together, and his faith was made complete by what he did. And the scripture was fulfilled that says, 'Abraham believed God, and it was credited to him as righteousness,' and he was called God's friend. You see that a person is justified by what he does and not by faith alone. In the same way, was not even Rahab the prostitute considered righteous for what she did when she gave lodging to the spies and sent them off in a different direction? As the body without the spirit is dead, so faith without deeds is dead."

In Ephesians, too, we read that it is not our own works that save us. We can see that faith is real when acted on for Jesus, but that it is not the actions themselves, or ourselves that save us. Only Christ saves! Paul writes to the Church in Ephesus and reminds them (and us), "For it is by grace you have been saved, through faith - and this not from yourselves, it is the gift of God - not by works, so that no one can boast" (Ephesians 2:8-9).

65. Letting Christ's love naturally shine through us was mentioned in the Introduction to this book. You can

Notes

read that, and also Matthew 5:13-18, which includes, "You are the light of the world. A city on a hill cannot be hidden" (Matthew 5:14). In Christ, we naturally reflect His light. The verse does not say, "Try really hard to show the light," but rather, "You are the light." 2 Corinthians 9:7-8 describes, "Each man should give what he has decided in his heart to give, not reluctantly or under compulsion, for God loves a cheerful giver. And God is able to make all grace abound to you, so that in all things at all times, having all that you need, you will abound in every good work." God is the One who provides the light; all we have do is joyfully reflect Him. Let's remember who we are in Christ and provide His love to others, naturally!

66. (Continue reading for the Spaghetti recipe's footnote!) Like anything with great outcomes, cooking steak takes practice! You'll have to work with your own grill, weather, thickness of cut, and flame intensity to get it just right. I would recommend though, this general process of searing the outside first, 3-4 minutes per side. The cooked outer layer makes sure that all the juices stay inside when finishing the steak at a lowered temperature. In effect, it somewhat steams the inside. When you feel it's done, cut into the midsection to see if you need more time. Make sure that it's all pink or brown, and not purple, as that is still not quite cooked yet. Just put it on a few more minutes if it needs it. Praise God for the results of patience! (1 Timothy 1:16; Galatians 5:22; James 5:10)

Taking the steak off the grill just a little before it's done helps with flavor and juiciness. Cover it with foil and let it sit for about 7 minutes. With tacos, it is also nice to cut all the meat into strips before serving. This will really work on your hand muscles and leave you lots more juice on the plate. Sometimes I use the juice as a topping for the tacos or as a dipping sauce for the steak the next day! Have fun experimenting and getting the steak cooked just right! Remember that in all things God can teach you lessons, even if they seem monotonous or mundane. When times seem more tedious too, you're probably doing something with Him that is very important! Anything that He is doing in your life is training you for loving Him and others better! I recently read a footnote on Psalm 134:1 which says, "Praise the LORD, all you servants of the LORD who minister by night in the house of the LORD." The footnote described how the Levites served as temple watchmen. They would stay up all night to make sure the temple was safe. There job may not have gotten much glory, and it was probably monotonous, but they did it as an act of worship to God. The Psalmist recorded their service as something praiseworthy![a] And think about Ecclesiastes 7:13, which says, "Consider what God has done: Who can straighten what he has made crooked? When times are good, be happy; but when times are bad, consider: God has made the one as well as the other. Therefore, a man cannot discover anything about his future." God gives you all types of different lessons. They may seem really hard at times, but everything can be used for His good. Just read Joseph's story. He was sold into slavery by his brothers, but because of that hardship, he was enabled by God (and only by God), to save them and all of Egypt from a seven year famine (see more on 'Spaghetti,' pg. 71). Plus, God showed His faithfulness by keeping His promise to Abraham, Isaac and Jacob, in that He would establish their descendents forever (see 'b'). Genesis 22:15-18 records, "The angel of the LORD called to Abraham from heaven a second time and said, "I swear by myself, declares the LORD, that because you have done this and have not withheld your son, your only son, I will surely bless you and make your descendants as numerous as the stars in the sky and as the sand on the seashore. Your descendants will take possession of the cities of their enemies, and through your offspring all nations on earth will be blessed, because you have obeyed me." The LORD's promise came true when the Israelites, descendents of Abraham, Isaac and Jacob, were kept alive during the famine. I would encourage you to read all of Joseph's story, for it is so amazing, and evident how God is at work. All of God's promises are kept true, and He is using you today to help Him live out His Sovereign plan! Trust that what He is doing in your life is worth it, because it is!

a. See commentary on 134:1-3, pg. 1053
Life Application Bible: New International Version. Wheaton And Grand Rapids: Tyndale House Publishers, Inc. and Zondervan, 1991. 1053. Print.

b. Here are several times when God promises them (Abraham, Isaac and Jacob) that there descendents will last forever by Himself, God alone: Genesis 22:15-18, Genesis 26:3-4 and Genesis 28:13-1. All these promises were true and shown to be true! Also, there are many more 'prophesies,' a little bit different, in the Old Testament that come true. Prophecies are sometimes predictions about future events, or simply God's Word spoken, both of which the Holy Spirit guides someone in telling (for example, see Psalm 41; Isaiah 42; 53:4-7, and footnotes 51 and 67). Plus, everything Jesus says is true!

67. The chapter headers in my Bible give some history, audience information, writer biographies, and maps of where Jesus went and where His miracles took place.[a] Here are a few insights my Bible's commentators had into not only the above details, but also general analysis of *why* the four Gospel writers wrote their accounts. The actual Gospels themselves give the full version, and it is easy to see the themes, but these notes are more simplified! Enjoy learning about God from these four amazingly

unique yet similar perspectives. Hallelujah!

The Gospel according to Matthew was written by a disciple of Jesus. He was originally a tax collector and disliked by many people. Jesus received him with open arms though, and eventually Matthew changed his ways to became a true follower and student of Christ. Matthew wrote about how Jesus is the Messiah ('the Anointed One' in Hebrew and 'Christ' in Greek). Jesus came as the Savior, (Jesus means *the LORD saves!*) and was the Messiah, but didn't act the way people thought that He would.[tb] Most of the people thought that He would be a military leader, giving them relief from their current oppression by the Roman government. Jesus set people free from much more though! He offers to set people free from the oppression of sin and death forever! He came as a leader of a Kingdom that will never be shaken! Matthew wrote these testaments to mostly Jews who had long been awaiting the prophecy that Jesus would be a descendent out of the line of David (and also that He would fulfil all the other prophecies and be the Messiah). That is why Matthew starts with the genealogy in verses 1:1-17, showing the line and the prophesies to be coming true! (Some prophecies for Jesus as a descendant of David are recorded in (1) Isaiah 9:6-7; (2) Isaiah 10:33-11:1 where Judah, who is the royal line of David, would be like the trees cut down, but then the Messiah, Jesus, would rise as a shoot from the stump; (3) Jeremiah 23:5-7; (4) 2 Samuel 7:11-16 about Jesus coming to be the LORD Himself who, "will establish a house for you:" (2 Samuel 7:11), and (5) Acts 2:22-41. For more prophecies about Jesus, see Matthew 1:22-23; 2; 3:3; 4:15-16; and read footnote 66b!) The prophecies all point to Jesus being the Messiah, or 'the Anointed One' coming to save everyone from their sins! I would recommend reading all the above passages and realizing that Jesus' coming was truly predicted. The records really show the events happened and furthermore that Jesus is risen! Matthew portrayed these and other miracles in a non-chronological order, instead organizing them to express how *Jesus is the Messiah*. He included the miracles to show *Christ's authority* and to culminate in *His victory* over sin and death forever! Praise God!

The Gospel according to Mark was written by John Mark. "He was not one of the 12 disciples but he accompanied Paul on his first missionary journey."[tc] Thus, he was credible. He wrote about how Jesus is the Messiah, and emphasized the personhood of Jesus. *Jesus is fully God and fully human; it's a miracle!* He is God in the flesh. John Mark also wrote about the work and teachings of Jesus. He mostly wrote to the Christians in Rome, who had lots of wealth. That is why he portrayed Jesus' personhood, work and teachings through *miracles* and *service*. In fact, there are more miracles recorded in Mark than in the other Gospels. Mark was showing that Jesus, although He was a person, was also God, and that God works miracles of healing emotionally, physically, spiritually; in every form. God heals the whole person and *doesn't reject anyone*. "No one was rejected or ignored by him."[td] Secondly, Mark recorded how Jesus teaches all of us to depend on Him to serve others. It is not what we have in possessions that matters, but how our hearts depend on Him. Mark included the verse in 10:43-45 when Jesus said, "Not so with you. Instead, whoever wants to become great among you must be your servant, and whoever wants to be first must be slave of all. For even the Son of Man did not come to be served, but to serve, and to give his life as a ransom for many." (Jesus' Word to us here was also recorded by Matthew in verses 20:26-28. The phrasing is almost exactly the same. Remember, at this time, quotations were more often memorized rather than written, so it is amazing that what these writers recorded was so strikingly similar. Jesus had a large impact on people.) The emphasis of service showed that Jesus gave in abundance to the Christians in Rome *so that they could bless others*! For, we are continually filled by Him to fill others (something my pastor, Josh White, always reminds)! These two themes showed that Jesus was the only true source of worth. It was not because they had a lot that they were saved. It was *only through Jesus that they could be saved*. Amen! He is Good! (The steak tacos recipe focuses on service and that is how it relates to the Gospel of Mark!)

The Gospel of Luke was written by a doctor, who was another friend of Paul. Luke wrote about Christ as the perfect human *Savior*. Thus, Luke also pointed to Jesus' humanity and divine nature miracle. Luke was writing to everyone though, including Gentiles (any non-Jews). Influenced by his audience and his gift as a doctor, he included many *details about Jesus*, and details on the context for people's physical ailments. He wrote to explain how Jesus is the *Savior for everyone*, not just the Jews and/ or physically healthy. In fact, Luke 5:31-32 records, "Jesus answered them, 'It is not the healthy who need a doctor, but the sick. I have not come to call the righteous, but sinners to repentance.'" (Jesus Word here was also recorded in Matthew 9:12-13 and Mark 2:17!) Everyone needs the Savior, and Jesus offers to save us *all*! Additionally, Luke records Jesus' promise of the Holy Spirit to be available to us all. All we have to do is humbly receive Him. Luke records this promise in verses 24:1-53. (The promise of the Holy Spirit, or 'Counselor,' is also recorded in John 14:16, 26; 15:26; 16:7, and the verses surrounding them. He is shown elsewhere throughout Scripture, too, such as in Acts 2:1-4!) Jesus made sure that we all had access to <u>Him</u> and the <u>Father</u>, through the <u>Holy Spirit</u>, that we all knew that the Three are One, and wanted all of us to know Him personally! Praise God! (The unity of the Holy Trinity is revealed in: Matthew 28:19-20 with the singular 'Name,' pointed to in the first verses of the Gospel according to John, and referenced all throughout Scripture. To read more on the Holy Trinity relationship, look at footnotes 47 and 75.) Thank God for revealing Himself through Luke!

Notes

The Gospel according to John was written by John the apostle, brother of James. He wrote about Jesus to show that He was the *true Son of God*, and that *all who believe in Him are saved, plus have eternal life with Jesus!* John was writing to new Christians and said the facts like they were. One of the most quoted verses of Scripture is John 3:16 (and 17). They say, "For God so loved the world that he gave his one and only Son, that whoever believe in him shall not perish but have eternal life. For God did not send his Son into the world to condemn the world, but to save the world through him." Jesus really offers salvation! This verse is quoted so much because it simply states the truth! Jesus Loves and saves! (*Jesus* even means *the LORD saves!*) John also included eight major miracles to display Jesus' divine nature. (John emphasized Jesus' divine nature, but still included His humanity, whereas Mark and Luke focused more on His human nature, but gave examples of His divinity; Matthew focused on Jesus being the Messiah as predicted by prophecy and seemed to balance Jesus' nature. That is what I think though. See for yourself. I would love to hear from you!) Of these eight miracles, six of them are unique to the Gospel according to John, and actually, according to my Bible, 90% of John is unique to John. This includes the 'Upper Room discourse' in chapters 14-17.[te] Even with just these eight miracles, we can see that Jesus is LORD!!! Here is a list of these miracles and their verses: "(1) turning water to wine (2:1-11), (2) healing the official's son (4:46-54), (3) healing the invalid at Bethesda (5:1-9), (4) feeding the 5,000 with just a few loaves and fish (6:1-14), (5) walking on the water (6:15-21), (6) restoring sight to the blind man (9:1-41), (7) raising Lazarus from the dead (11:1-44), and, after the resurrection, (8) giving the disciples an overwhelming catch of fish (21:1-14)."[tf] I would encourage all of us to read and re-read them! They are all so packed with meaning, healing, insight, teaching, and Jesus' love! He is here!

John also gave many examples of Jesus *revealing His identity*. Jesus showed to us that He is the way and the truth and the life (John 14:6), and referred to Himself with an "I am" pattern (as noted by my Bible's commentary). Jesus referring to Himself with this pattern would make sense because He is God, and He is the same God that appeared so long ago to Moses in the burning bush. At that time, when Moses asked Him His Name, "God said to Moses, 'I AM WHO I AM. This is what you are to say to the Israelites: I AM has sent me to you'" (Exodus 3:14). Jesus always has the same Character and is God forever (read more in footnote 47)! So, the pattern may seem insignificant, but is actually a big deal! Here are several more passages when Jesus declares His identity, and further expands our view of His gloriously deep Character: "Jesus says, *I am* the bread of life (6:35); *I am* the light of the world (8:12; 9:5); *I am* the gate (10:7); *I am* the good shepherd (10:11, 14); *I am* the resurrection and the life (11:25); *I am* the way the truth and the life (14:6); and *I am* the true vine (15:1)."[tf] God's Holy Character is what our hearts were made for (pg. 113). Only He can bring us to Him, and only He can fulfil our needs!

John concludes with the resurrection account, the great miracle of *Jesus raising from the dead to defeat death and sin forever!* And John records Jesus promising the *Holy Spirit*, to His disciples and to all of us, in place of Him physically (Jesus says 'Counselor'). This means that Jesus can now be with all of us at once by the Holy Spirit! What a sacrifice and gift! Some verses that record Jesus promising the Holy Spirit, and talking about Him, are in John 14:16, 26; 15:26; 16:7; and surrounding verses.

68.　　　These events and Gospels point to Jesus being: our Savior, real, loving, truthful, healing, consistent in Character, and God! The four Gospels all give slightly different perspectives because they were from unique people, but at the same time, they all convey the same, essential truth: Jesus! He is the way and truth and life to save us! When the Gospels are read together, they give a more complete view of Him.

What has God done in your life? God has given you opportunities as a testimony to share His Gospel in a unique way that will tell people about Him! Share what God has given you and it will move others and you to know Him more as you are fully known (1 Corinthians 13:12-13, and preceding verses)!

a. My Bible was given to me as a gift from Carol Steele, a true friend and sister in Christ! It is called the 'Life Application Bible,' and I would actually really recommend getting it. The resources in the footnotes and chapter headers give great insights and introductions into the Scripture! The Bible is sited below. Praise God for His Word who is Jesus (John 1:1-2, 14-18)!

b. See footnotes b and c, respectively, pgs. 1640 and 1641

c. See 'Vital Statistics' in the Introduction to the Gospel according to Mark, pg. 1722

d. This footnote was actually in 'Megathemes' under 'Compassion' in the Introduction to the Gospel according to Luke, but was fitting to include in the section on Mark. Jesus offers forgiveness to all! pg. 1783

e. See 'Special Features' under 'Vital Statistics' in the Introduction to the Gospel according to John, pg. 1866

f. See the fourth-to-last and third-to-last paragraphs, respectively, in the Introduction to the Gospel according to John, pg. 1866

Life Application Bible: New International Version. Wheaton And Grand Rapids: Tyndale House Publishers, Inc. and Zondervan, 1991. 1640 and 1641; 1722; 1783; and 1866; respectively. Print.

Notes

69. There are about 50,000 to 200,000 SHU's for a rocoto pepper or a habenero pepper. There are only a handful more peppers in the world that are hotter. SHU's, or Scoville heat units, were first developed by Wilbur Scoville to relate the amount of capsaicin present, based on a, "none present to pure capsaicin present" scale. (This scale is subjective, however, and is only for a general measure of 'spiciness.') Measured on the scale, these peppers are at least ten times hotter than serrano peppers, which are still really spicy! To compare, serrano peppers are at least three times hotter than jalapeño peppers and ten times hotter than bell peppers. No wonder something was different! With the same thought, let's live differently for Jesus, and not settle for bland (and you may not like spice, so instead think of something with no taste, or something really tasty)! God said in Leviticus and elsewhere, "I am the LORD who brought you up out of Egypt to be your God; therefore be holy, because I am holy" (Leviticus 11:45; also all throughout Scripture, and referrenced in 1 Peter 1:16). *Let's be holy set apart for God, naturally (see footnote 65)!*

70. My pastor spoke on purity several times. He describes *pure* as, "not only cleansing but *singleness*, or *without mixture.*" Thus, purity is not just trying to live by the rules, it is rather living fully for Christ with Him in us and us in Him! I would encourage you to listen to both sermons and *receive* God's purity!

    White, Josh, narr. "Why Simplicity" The Four Pillars. Door of Hope, under God's direction, Portland, 26 Sept. 2011. Web. 16 Nov. 2011. <http://www.doorofhopepdx.org/media/teachings/category/the-four-pillars.html>.

    (See this mostly) White, Josh, narr. "The Pure in Heart" The Beatitudes. Door of Hope, under God's direction, Portland, 14 Nov. 2011. Web. 16 Nov. 2011. <http://www.doorofhopepdx.org/media/teachings/category/the-beatitudes.html>.

71. Jesus said, "What goes into a man's mouth does not make him 'unclean,' but what comes out of his mouth, that is what makes him 'unclean'" (Matthew 15:11). Jesus shows that it is not the food, or anything religious that we do, that changes us. It is all of us: our heart, mind, soul, and strength *with Him*, that matters (Luke 10:27). And *He* changes us from the inside out to do His work, and to save us. This change does not come from us! It is His gift! In John 14:6, "Jesus answered, "I am the way and the truth and the life. No one comes to the Father except through me." Praise the LORD that *He saves us*!!!

72. 1 cup of raw quinoa will yield about 3 cups of cooked quinoa because of the water intake. To make the quinoa, first rinse and then put in a large pot (or rice maker) with twice the amount of water or fat-strained broth. Cover and simmer for 10-15 minutes, then let cool. Add all the other ingredients and flavor to taste.

It's really that simple, and so is Jesus' friendship! He already died for us, so let's trust in Him and live, because He lives! (For flavoring the quinoa, use the spices noted on the page and some olive oil. I often put in more cilantro and lime than anything else. To read more about cooking quinoa and broths, see: 'Sabrina's Quinoa Salad,' pg. 45, and footnote 40, respectively. To read about the health benefits of quinoa see 'An Introduction to Proteins and Amino Acids,' pg. 17. It's a real blessing from the LORD!)

73. The peppers will slightly golden and char. You can either carefully rotate them with grill tongs, or just leave them be. Don't worry if the bottoms are more charred than the sides because time adds flavor and texture. You can discard the very bottom when eating the peppers. Remember too that Jesus said, "I have told you these things, so that in me you may have peace. In this world you will have trouble. But take heart! I have overcome the world" (John 16:33).

74. See *shish kebab* and *kebab*, respectively:
Harper, Douglas. Online Etymology Dictionary. Douglas Harper, n.d. Web. 21 Dec. 2011.
<http://www.etymonline.com/index.php?allowed_in_frame=0&search=shish&searchmode=none>.

75. Jesus and His love are really deep! For example, Jesus was once talking to a Samaritan woman, which was not culturally proper. But God came down to our level and loves all of us where we are at, no matter the world's cultural differences. Jesus talked to her and later revealed that He was the Messiah, or 'Anointed One' (called Christ). She and everyone had been waiting for Him. Here is the part where she still does not recognize who He is. John records, "'Sir,' the woman said, 'you have nothing to draw with and the well is deep. Where can you get this living water? Are you greater than our father Jacob, who gave us the well and drank from it himself, as did also his sons and his flocks and herds?' Jesus answered, 'Everyone who drinks this water will be thirsty again, but whoever drinks the water I give him will never thirst. Indeed, the water I give him will become in him a spring of water welling up to eternal life'" (John 4:11-14; I would also recommend reading the surrounding verses. They are beautiful because they are His Words of life (John 1:1)!) Jesus and His Words to us are deep; in fact, *there is no end to His depth and Character!* When we learn more about other cultures, spend time with His people, and listen, then we can learn more about Him too. As we can see in this story, He offered His life for all people! However, Jesus and God and the Holy Spirit are One! There is no God other than *God.* When we spend time with other cultures, we cannot think that He should be changed or reduced just to fit in. Consider the greatest commandment as recorded in Deuteronomy 6:4-5, "Hear, O Israel: The LORD our God, the LORD is one. Love the LORD your God with all your heart and with all your

Notes

soul and with all your strength" (In Mark, Jesus quotes this verse and includes, "mind" to show that we should be completely about loving God first, and then our neighbors second). God is One. In all parts of Scripture we read this message. Here are a few other verses that also reveal how God is the One true God: (1) Deuteronomy 4:35, "You were shown these things so that you might know that the LORD is God; besides him there is no other." (This is when God alone was bringing the Israelites out of Egypt with a mighty hand and outstretched arm, performing many miracles for them, and providing for them in the desert); (2) 1 Samuel 2:2, "There is no one holy like the LORD; there is no one besides you; there is no Rock like our God", and (3) God Himself saying that He is the, "Only God" several times. As recorded in Isaiah 44:8, "Do not tremble, do not be afraid. Did I not proclaim this and foretell it long ago? You are my witnesses. Is there any God besides me? No, there is no other Rock; I know not one." Also, Jesus refers to the Three-In-One Name in Matthew 28:19-20, when He says, "Therefore go and make disciples of all nations, baptizing them in the <u>name</u> of the Father and of the Son and of the Holy Spirit, and teaching them to obey everything I have commanded you. And surely I am with you always, to the very end of the age." In many many many places Jesus/ God/ the Holy Spirit declare that there is only One God, that being Him! Hallelujah! (God's Holy Name and His Trinity relationship is also discussed in footnote 47!)

We can see, too, that *God's Character is unchanging.* He originally said to Moses in the burning bush, as recorded in Exodus 3:14, "I AM WHO I AM. This is what you are to say to the Israelites: 'I AM has sent me to you.'" And, in John 14:6 Jesus uses this same pattern: "Jesus answered, "I am the way and the truth and the life. No one comes to the Father except through me." Jesus was God in the flesh, so He used the same pattern of "I AM" (Also, Jesus is the way and the truth and the life! Hallelujah that He died so we don't have to!) When we are with other cultures, there may be interesting things to learn about Jesus' love, like how to care for people better, but that does not mean that we can change God. God is God. The LORD wants us to *engage* with all people as He did, but not to start practicing anything their culture does that goes against Him and His Word! God calls us to be holy, or *set apart,* for Him. Here are a few verse about being holy: (1) John 15:19, "If you belonged to the world, it would love you as its own. As it is, you do not belong to the world, but I have chosen you out of the world. That is why the world hates you."; (2) 1 Timothy 6:7, "For we brought nothing into the world, and we can take nothing out of it."; (3) Romans 12:2, "Do not conform any longer to the pattern of this world, but be transformed by the renewing of your mind. Then you will be able to test and approve what God's will is - his good, pleasing and perfect will.", and (4) Leviticus 11:45, "I am the LORD who brought you up out of

Egypt to be your God; therefore be holy, because I am holy." Therefore, let's be *holy*. And furthermore, let's be *lovingly holy*. For remember, in Romans 2:4 Paul writes, "Or do you show contempt for the riches of his kindness, tolerance and patience, not realizing that God's kindness leads you toward repentance?" It's God's kindness that leads us towards repentance, so when you see someone doing something wrong, show them Jesus' love, and point them to Him *in His love*.

P.S. That was essentially a long way of saying the greatest commandments. As recorded in Mark, "'The most important one,' answered Jesus, 'is this: 'Hear, O Israel, the Lord our God, the Lord is <u>one</u>. Love the Lord your God with all your heart and with all your soul and with all your mind and with all your strength. The second is this: 'Love your neighbor as yourself.' There is no commandment greater than these'" (Mark 12:29-31). I just thought it was important to share that loving people from the American viewpoint is not true, but loving people in Christ's way is true and real. Christ's way loves all people and all cultures because He alone is God! He is the One and Only Way! (John 14:6).

76. Lewis, C.S. Mere Christianity. N.p.: n.p., 1952. 30. google: full-proof.org. Web. 22 Nov. 2011. <http://www.full-proof.org/wp-content/uploads/2010/04/Mere-Christianity-Lewis-chapters.pdf>.

77. Jesus is the way! He said in John 14:6, "I am the way and the truth and the life. No one comes to the Father except through me." <u>Jesus is the way, and there is no other!</u> It is interesting to note, too, that Jesus is the Word of God in the flesh. As recorded in John 1:14, "The Word became flesh and made his dwelling among us. We have seen his glory, the glory of the One and Only,† who came from the Father, full of grace and truth." Jesus is God's Word to us, so when He says things, as recorded in Scripture, they are trustworthy, true and filling! They are from Him, or of Him (*He is the Word*)! Also, Jesus quotes many Old Testament Scriptures and explains that the meaning behind any Law or prophecy was Him, and His message of loving Him and others more (Matthew 5:17; see also footnotes 51, 66b and 67 for prophecies). Plus, consider 2 Timothy 3:16, which says, "All Scripture is God-breathed and is useful for teaching, rebuking, correcting and training in righteousness, so that the man of God may be thoroughly equipped for every good work." God's Word to us is revealed in Jesus and recorded in the Bible! Let's daily learn to love Him and others more by marinating in His 'recipes' and eating His Word (John 6:35). For we cannot live or love without Him living and loving in us.

For the steak: To start the steak, marinate it for an hour to a day. When having just steak with potatoes, try using: red pepper flakes, marjoram, some chili powder, and cayenne pepper, lime and

†*Or the Only Begotten*

cilantro (on occasion because they do make it different), minced garlic cloves, red onions, and olive oil. I prefer to start with the spices, so that they better adhere to the meat, then add the vegetables, and finish with the citrus and olive oil (for more information on this method look to footnote 66). There are many ways to marinate steaks though. For a Mexican flavor, read 'Kale Steak,' footnote 60, and of course, you can try different ingredients and spices all together!

For the potatoes: To make the potatoes, simply cube and boil for about 45 minutes in plenty of water. Add: oregano, marjoram, Italian seasoning, lemon juice (about 1/4 lemon), a bay leaf, a dash of basil and 1 Tbsp extra virgin olive oil. When soft, take the potatoes out and mash in a bowl. Combine with: 1/4 cup milk, 3-4 chopped garlic cloves, some basil, green onions, and olive oil. You can also add some chopped carrots if you'd like. This method adds exceptional flavor to the potatoes during the boiling process, and requires neither salt nor butter! (Some other methods to make the potatoes include baking them in the oven at 350°F for about 1 hour, or microwaving them on high heat for about 10 minutes.)

For the sides: To make a side, such as asparagus, green beans, broccoli, or broccolini, first wash them. With the asparagus and broccoli/ broccolini, cut off the bottoms of the stalks or stems as these are more fibrous and bitter. Then, throw all into a pan with olive oil, lemon juice and spices (such as Italian seasoning, marjoram, red and black pepper). Sear on high heat for approximately 5 minutes until slightly charred. Near the end, add 3-4 chopped garlic cloves and/ or slivered almonds. Cook a little longer and you're ready to go! O prova (*or try it*) all'agro, by blanching and serving with lemon, olive oil and pepper.[89a] Boil for a few minutes, then plunge into ice water to arrest the cooking process. For more on vegetable appetizers, see 'Broccolini e Asparagi,' pg. 36.

With all of these preparations remember the One who made us, Who completes us, and Who is the answer (Mark 12:29-31)! Acts 17:28 records, "'For in him we live and move and have our being.' As some of your own poets have said, 'We are his offspring.'"

78. There are many places in Scripture where Jesus describes and shows that He is fulfilling the Law and Prophets. These include Him being the long awaited Messiah, Hebrew for 'Anointed One,' come to save people - Jesus means *the LORD saves*! (Jesus as Messiah can be read in numerous verses including Acts 2:22-41 and Luke 9:18-20, but for the specific prophecy of Him being a dependent of David, read Matthew 1-2:12 and footnote 51.) This is what the first pizza recipe represents: Jesus fulfilling prophecy. In addition, it represents Him laying a firm foundation for the future (consider the second pizza recipe). There are many promises Jesus makes for when *He comes back*, and He will fulfil all these just as He has fulfilled all the others! For, "Now we see but a poor reflection as in a mirror; then we shall see face to

face. Now I know in part; then I shall know fully, even as I am fully known" (1 Corinthians 13:12). Jesus will return one day! He describes, "Heaven and earth will pass away, but my words will never pass away. 'No one knows about that day or hour, not even the angels in heaven, nor the Son, but only the Father. As it was in the days of Noah, so it will be at the coming of the Son of Man" (Matthew 24:35-37). Let's re-read the surrounding verses. It is so clear that He is returning, and He is so clear about it! He wants us to know so that we won't miss Him. We have to be with Him when He returns though. Let's not live like those in Noah's time and ignore His Word to us! (See also footnote 47's note.)

In Acts 1:10-11, Paul also records, "They were looking intently up into the sky as he was going, when suddenly two men dressed in white stood beside them. 'Men of Galilee,' they said, 'why do you stand here looking into the sky? This same Jesus, who has been taken from you into heaven, will come back in the same way you have seen him go to heaven.'" There is more to fulfil until His heaven comes on earth, but the foundation He laid while He was here the first time was not in vain. Jesus completes and fulfils everything, and will continue to do so until all things are for Him! Revelation 5:19-10 speaks of His heaven on earth: "And they sang a new song: 'You are worthy to take the scroll and to open its seals, because you were slain, and with your blood you purchased men for God from every tribe and language and people and nation. You have made them to be a kingdom and priests to serve our God, and they will reign on the earth.'" Jesus is LORD, now and forever!

Jesus mentions returning and the kingdom of heaven in some other verses too. Aside from (1) Matthew 24:1-25:46, here are a few others: (2) Mark 13:1-37; (3) Luke 17:20-37 ([1-3] are all on the end times); (4) Matthew 13:1-52, which is His parable relating the kingdom of heaven to sowing seed, (see also Mark 4:1-34, the amazing things in verses 34-41, and Luke 8:1-18); (5) Luke 14:15-23; (6) John 8:21-30; and also (7) Daniel 9:27, 11:3, and 12:11, on how the daily sacrifice will be abolished.

It would be great to read all these verses and see that He *is* planning on returning; His promise *will* be kept just like any other! Let's live for Him now and forever! Remember in the process, He will protect and set free. Romans 8:1-2, reminds, "Therefore, there is now no condemnation for those who are in Christ Jesus, because through Christ Jesus the law of the Spirit of life set me free from the law of sin and death." In Christ Jesus we are set alive and free to be with Him in His Good Kingdom forever! Only in Christ, and not of ourselves, has this been made possible (see below)!

79. Galatians 5:13 says, "You, my brothers, were called to be free. But do not use your freedom to indulge the sinful nature; rather, serve one another in love." Jesus set us free to love Him and others. You have heard that it was said (a phrase Jesus uses), that the greatest commandment is to, "Love the Lord

your God with all your heart and with all your soul and with all your mind and with all your strength" (Mark 12:30) and, "The second is this: 'Love your neighbor as yourself.' There is no commandment greater than these" (Mark 12:31). This is so important that it's repeated all throughout Scripture, for example, in Galatians 5:13-14. God's Word to us says it so clearly. We are to live for God and others, and He sets us free to do that! Amen! Here are the words of Paul, inspired by God: "You, my brothers, were called to be free. But do not use your freedom to indulge the sinful nature; rather, serve one another in love. The entire law is summed up in a single command: 'Love your neighbor as yourself.' If you keep on biting and devouring each other, watch out or you will be destroyed by each other. So I say, live by the Spirit, and you will not gratify the desires of the sinful nature. For the sinful nature desires what is contrary to the Spirit, and the Spirit what is contrary to the sinful nature. They are in conflict with each other, so that you do not do what you want. But if you are led by the Spirit, you are not under law. The acts of the sinful nature are obvious: sexual immorality, impurity and debauchery; idolatry and witchcraft; hatred, discord, jealousy, fits of rage, selfish ambition, dissensions, factions and envy; drunkenness, orgies, and the like. I warn you, as I did before, that those who live like this will not inherit the kingdom of God. But the fruit of the Spirit is love, joy, peace, patience, kindness, goodness, faithfulness, gentleness and self-control. Against such things there is no law. Those who belong to Christ Jesus have crucified the sinful nature with its passions and desires. Since we live by the Spirit, let us keep in step with the Spirit. Let us not become conceited, provoking and envying each other" (Galatians 5:13-26).

80. When you look at any of the multiple Old Testament prophecies coming true (to start, see some fulfilments in Jesus, recorded in: Matthew 1:1-17, 22-23; 2:5-6, 14-15, 17-18; 3:3; 4:15-16, as well as footnotes 51, 66b and 67) you can see that Jesus is *always* trustworthy and *always* faithful! These and all other promises can *only be fulfilled with Him and in Him*. Jesus is so worthy! He is God! (See also Isaiah 53!)

   There are many other verses that express His faithfulness, too. Psalm 33:4 and Psalm 111:7 are some great and poetic examples. Psalm 33:4 sings, "For the word of the LORD is right and true; he is faithful in all he does." And Psalm 111:7 exonerates, "The works of his hands are faithful and just; all his precepts are trustworthy." Consider making your own praises to God as well for all the times that He has been faithful to you. When you start to think about it, God is always faithful!!! Praise Him!

81. recipe for the pizza sauce, pgs. 90 or 114, but with the Mexican spices and less reduction. Fill the tortillas with the remaining ingredients, tightly wrap and place into a baking pan. Cover the tops with more sauce and assorted enchilada cheeses. Bake for about 10 minutes until golden! Then, taking in the warm and

terrific smells, garnish it up with cilantro, guacamole (pg. 121), limes, even sunflower seeds, and of course, hot sauce to taste. Get ready for 'being comfortable with being uncomfortable,'[a] and enjoy the surprisingly spicy yet refreshing treat in food and Him!

a. 'Being comfortable with being uncomfortable' is something that a new friend of mine, Leah, just mentioned the other night at a Bible study. Everyone there had read the verses in Matthew 5:10-12 and Acts 5:17-42, and we were all amazed at the obedience of God's apostles! Leah's statement exactly describes the inner change that needs to take place in all of us. By the world's standards, sharing God with someone, or speaking about what Jesus has done for us, may seem uncomfortable, or even offensive - offensive because we all have sinned, not because God is not loving, or we are being rude to them. Fortunately though, Jesus came to save us, and set us free from condemnation! (Rom 8:1-2) Only by putting away our selfish desires, can there be room to have Him in us. Therefore, let's all live for Him and lovingly tell others because the small cost of opposition now is worth someone knowing Jesus forever. Let's also *let Jesus work through us, so that it is Him whom people are meeting with, and so that we may not be burdened.* (For example, it's not arguments that saves people, it's Jesus who saves!) Matthew 11:28-30 says, "Come to me, all you who are weary and burdened, and I will give you rest. Take my yoke upon you and learn from me, for I am gentle and humble in heart, and you will find rest for your souls. For my yoke is easy and my burden is light." Hallelujah for Jesus! He is the only way (John 14:6), and He has victory (1 Corinthians 15:55-58; 1 John 5:4)! (Plus, remember, Jesus *kindly* saves us! Paul reminds the Church in Rome: "Or do you show contempt for the riches of his kindness, tolerance and patience, not realizing that God's kindness leads you toward repentance?" (Romans 2:4). It's God's kindness that leads us to Him, so we should treat others the same way if God is really living in us! Romans 12:18 also says, "If it is possible, as far as it depends on you, live at peace with everyone." By letting God's love in us, our friends can see *His love*, and receive *His peace*. Only He can set us free; we just share!) (See also footnote 86, and 'Rhubarbara Pie,' pg. 124 for context!)

82. On the site below, there are some great insights into Jesus' Beatitudes recorded in Matthew 5:1-12.[a] They are teachings on each Beatitude from my Church, Door of Hope. By looking to Jesus and what He did, we can see the best example of these Beatitudes lived out. Additionally, here is the site for . . .

a. White, Josh, and Josh Wilder, narr. "Try to listen to all eight!" The Beatitudes. Door of Hope, under God's direction, Portland, 2011. Web. 25 Nov. 2011. <http://www.doorofhopepdx.org/media/teachings/category/the-beatitudes.html>.

all the teachings at Door of Hope.[b] Jesus has so much to share in His Word, and these teachings help to reveal His infinite love and depth! Enjoy learning more about Him, especially that He loved, loves and will always love us so! Praise God! (See 1 John 4:8, 16; John 3:16-17; 15:13!)

b. "Teachings." Door of Hope. N.p., 2011. Web. 25 Nov. 2011.
<http://www.doorofhopepdx.org/media/teachings.html>.

83. This verse is so cool! There is no shame for those who trust in Jesus! The next part of the verse is also very life-changing. Peter quotes from Psalm 118:22 and reminds us, "Now to you who believe, this stone is precious. But to those who do not believe, 'The stone the builders rejected has become the capstone'" (1 Peter 2:7). Jesus came to save and be the support for us. He is the foundational strength and essential piece that holds everything else together! (See footnote 85 as well.)

   Also, Peter was an apostle of Christ. The name *apostle* simply means *messenger* or someone *sent forth*[a] and in this case, by the Holy Spirit! We, too, can and should be apostles of Christ Jesus!

a. See *apostle*:
Harper, Douglas. Online Etymology Dictionary. Douglas Harper, n.d. Web. 25 Nov. 2011.
<http://www.etymonline.com/index.php?allowed_in_frame=0&search=apostle&searchmode=none>.

84. This is one of the only times that there is a suggested serving size. It can help you choose which cake pan to use, but really, we can always have enough because of Jesus (He is the bread of life; John 6:35)! Jesus shows that He can take any serving size and then multiply it to have enough for everyone to be well fed! You can read more in the recipe for bread and fish named, 'Luke 9:17' on pg. 85, and the passage in Luke 9:10-17. Actually, here it is: "When the apostles returned, they reported to Jesus what they had done. Then he took them with him and they withdrew by themselves to a town called Bethsaida, but the crowds learned about it and followed him. He welcomed them and spoke to them about the kingdom of God, and healed those who needed healing. Late in the afternoon the Twelve came to him and said, 'Send the crowd away so they can go to the surrounding villages and countryside and find food and lodging, because we are in a remote place here.' He replied, 'You give them some-thing to eat.' They answered, 'We have only five loaves of bread and two fish - unless we go and buy food for all this crowd.' (About five thousand men were there.) But he said to his disciples, 'Have them sit down in groups of about fifty each.' The disciples did so, and everybody sat down. Taking the five loaves and the two fish and looking up to heaven, he gave thanks and broke them. Then he gave them to the

disciples to set before the people. They all ate and were satisfied, and the disciples picked up twelve basketfuls of broken pieces that were left over."

85. (See footnote 83 as well!) Romans 8:31 says, "What, then, shall we say in response to this? If God is for us, who can be against us?" Even if it may seem that God is being unfair, His ways are higher than our ways. God says in Isaiah 55:9, "As the heavens are higher than the earth, so are my ways higher than your ways and my thoughts than your thoughts." The following verses are also very amazing. God continues with, "As the rain and the snow come down from heaven, and do not return to it without watering the earth and making it bud and flourish, so that it yields seed for the sower and bread for the eater, so is my word that goes out from my mouth: It will not return to me empty, but will accomplish what I desire and achieve the purpose for which I sent it. You will go out in joy and be led forth in peace; the mountains and hills will burst into song before you, and all the trees of the field will clap their hands. Instead of the thornbush will grow the pine tree, and instead of briers the myrtle will grow. This will be for the LORD's renown, for an everlasting sign, which will not be destroyed" (Isaiah 55:10-13).

The LORD says to us, "'For I know the plans I have for you,' declares the LORD, 'plans to prosper you and not to harm you, plans to give you hope and a future. Then you will call upon me and come and pray to me, and I will listen to you. You will seek me and find me when you seek me with all your heart. I will be found by you,' declares the LORD, 'and will bring you back from captivity. I will gather you from all the nations and places where I have banished you,' declares the LORD, 'and will bring you back to the place from which I carried you into exile'" (Jeremiah 29:11-14). Jesus is all for us! He has given us His love and *laid down His life* for us! Let's trust in Him, even if we can't quite see everything now, for He sees! Praise Him! (See also 'Sue's Chocolate Oatmeal Cake,' pg. 123.)

86. There is also a 'Marionberry Pie' (picture and Scripture on pg. 126), and an *Apple Crumb Pie*. It's a three-for-one deal, just like God, who is Three-in-One (footnotes 47 and 75)! May we put our faith in Him no matter what, for He has it figured out. Seriously, there is a reason that God had Barbara put those blueberries in, and that God had just a little left over for her. If we are willing to listen and be obedient, even when out of our comfort zones, then there will be so many moments like these!

To make the pie crust: Start by mixing the dry ingredients in a bowl. Add only a little bit at a time. Use two knives and criss cross, so the dough is mixed evenly while you clean the knives. Continuing to mix, add enough warm water (up to 2 Tbsp), so that the dough becomes floury, but not sticky. If you add too much water, you'll have to add more flour as well. Then the crust will turn tough and less flaky. Don't worry

Notes

if you don't get it right at first though (Matthew 6:25; Luke 12:22)! Jesus loves you so much!

Set aside a little more than half the dough for the bottom and keep the rest for the top. Shape each half with a rolling pin. Barbara had some really nice equipment to do so, such as a nonstick surface, a friction matt underneath, and a marble rolling pin. If you would like to make as many wonderful pies as she does, then I would recommend getting these. Otherwise, there is another method that will work just fine.

Add a little flour and water to the counter. Place some parchment paper on top. The flour and water combo is actually what made up the first glues, so it will prevent your paper from moving! Flour the parchment well, and set your dough there. Additionally, you can flour the top of the dough and use another layer of parchment to prevent your rolling pin from sticking. As you roll it out, add a little flour and flip to make sure it's going smoothly. Great!

Once the bottom and top crusts are rolled out, start to preheat your oven to 375°F (Barbara notes that if you use glass, the cooking temperature will be about 25°F lower than if you use ceramic or tin, which will bake the pies at 400°F). Then take the rolled-out bottom and carefully transfer it into a pie-baking pan. To do so, you can place the pie pan upside down over the dough, and turn the whole unit back over (with a cookie sheet underneath). With your fingers, gently make sure all the edges are conformed, and with a fork, prick all surfaces.

As seen in the photo, cut around the edge with a knife so that there is an even overlap. Fill the pie to the brim with your ingredients (to follow), and add the top rolled-out dough. To do so, fold it in half (dough side out over parchment), transfer to the pie, and roll back out. Afterwards, pinch the edges all the way around so that the pie is sealed. You can use any means of doing this. I have recently tried using my thumbs, one on each side, to press the outer edge into a wavy pattern. I noticed that when the pie cooks, the crust expands, so the waves become less pronounced. Therefore, exaggerate your edge. Finally, cut some slits in the top for ventilation and add any other decorative elements (such as hearts) with the remaining dough. Now you are ready for some fine smells! Brush the top generously with milk and sugar, and bake in the oven for 40-50 minutes. Start checking at 40 minutes in the top slits, to see how the filling is coming along.

To make the pie fillings!: (1) To make the 'Rhubarbara Pie,' pg. 124, add about 4 heaping cups rhubarb, 3/4 cup sugar, 4 Tbsp flour and 3-4 handfuls of blueberries on top. Start by mixing the flour and sugar and then combining both with the rhubarb. Flour helps to thicken any berry pie, and the taste of the rhubarb is complimented well by the sugar and blueberries. Add the rhubarb and blueberries in layers, with blueberries on top to finish, so that the juices combine. Also add some sugar to the top for good measure. Place the upper crust on and you're ready to go!

(2) To make the 'Marionberry Pie,' pg. 126, add about 4-5 cups berries, 3/4 cup sugar or less, 5 Tbsp flour and some corn starch. If you don't have Marionberries, then just use a berry medley. This is actually what I did for this pie picture, as it was out of season for Marionberries. Barbara recommends these layers: 2 1/2 cups blackberries on the bottom, sugar and corn starch next, 2 1/2 cups blueberries, sugar and corn starch, and 1 cup raspberries on top. This combination will give you a very merry bite.

(3) To make an *Apple Crumb Pie* use about 4-5 cups of apples, 1/2 cup sugar, and a little cinnamon. Barbara recommends getting the triad of Granny Smiths on the bottom, Golden Delicious in the middle, and Pink Lady's on the top. She notes that with the pectin in apples, there is no need for thickening layers. (Remember to be inventive with what you have!)

To make the *Apple Crumb* use 1/2 cup flour, 1/2 cup sugar and 2/3 cup butter or margarine (also see some replacement ideas below). Combine these ingredients in a similar manner as the pie crusts'. Enjoy Apple Pie with this delicious topping.

Barbara also wisely takes the scraps that are left over from the edges of the crust and bakes them as cinnamon strips or snikerdoodle-like strips. Roll out these left-overs into long rectangles and add your own topping. Bake for at least 30-40 minutes with the pie.

Thank God for Barbara and her pies, and thank God for the blueberries! The tart, raw flavor of the rhubarb is somewhat calmed by the baking process, but adding blueberries gives an amazing color and unbeatable flavor. Let's listen to Him leading us!

Have fun with the many recipes above. As God leads you in all cooking and creating in life, try variations and listen to what God has for you. For example, if you love the pie-making and eating experience, but would like to make it without butter or shortening, look to 'Chicken Pot Pie,' pg. 103 to start. The recipe's ratios are the same, but instead of the 1 1/3 cups shortening, it uses 1/3 cup sweet potato purée and 1 cup apple purée. Just boil the potato beforehand.

Finally, let's thank God for His rulers and authorities. As Paul wrote to the Romans, "Everyone must submit himself to the governing authorities, for there is no authority except that which God has established. The authorities that exist have been established by God" (Romans 13:1). When authorities are asking you to do something that is against God, then of course don't listen to them, and always follow God's leading first. Otherwise, let us submit to those who are in authority over us out of reverence for Christ. (Ephesians 5:21)

87. It seemed so evident to me that this marionberry pie resembled Jesus and His victory on the cross

for us. *Jesus died on the cross for our sins!* This is an expression of how much He loves us (John 15:13). Think about someone that you would lay down your life for. You probably are very close to them. Jesus is even closer! He died for our sins, so that we could have a right relationship with Him. Now, when we are before God, we are clean because Jesus took our place. Romans 8:1 reads, "Therefore, there is now no condemnation for those who are in Christ Jesus, because through Christ Jesus the law of the Spirit of life set me free from the law of sin and death." This is really good news.

Jesus is our best friend. As I saw this pie here on this winter day, the light, the color, the berries, everything made me think of Jesus and how He wants to be with us more and more. I really can see it now, whereas at first, the message was there and I could feel it, but it was not in words yet. The Holy Spirit had the words come so that you could hear about Him, instead of something from me. Let's all be baptised, and tell the world about Him as Jesus said, "Therefore go and make disciples of all nations, baptizing them in the name of the Father and of the Son and of the Holy Spirit, and teaching them to obey everything I have commanded you. And surely I am with you always, to the very end of the age." Everyone deserves to hear about Jesus in His Name!† That is why Jesus came. Let's do our job and share Him with others in Him, for He is doing His job to share. (See also 'Fruit,' pg. 128.)

For more on baptism too, listen to this great teaching from Door of Hope! May we be filled with His Spirit to tell others about Him and His love for them (†only by Him, in His Spirit, so people see *His* love)!

White, Josh, narr. "A Sacramental Cast" The Thinking Christian. Door of Hope, under God's direction, Portland, 13 Feb. 2012. Web. 17 Feb. 2012.
<http://www.doorofhopepdx.org/media/teachings/category/the-thinking-christian.html>.

88. Let's remain in Him!

89. garments, one being for a vest called an *ephod*. The fine materials helped the people to remember the Holiness and beauty that the LORD brings in life, specifically through any physical beauty (which is truly a blessing; and the vest was not the focus, but it pointed to the LORD, who is)! As instructed by the LORD, "They made the ephod of gold, and of blue, purple and scarlet yarn, and of finely twisted linen. They hammered out thin sheets of gold and cut strands to be worked into the blue, purple and scarlet yarn and fine linen - the work of a skilled craftsman. They made shoulder pieces for the ephod, which were attached to two of its corners, so it could be fastened. Its skilfully woven waistband was like it - of one piece with the ephod and made with gold, and with blue, purple and scarlet yarn, and with finely twisted linen, as the LORD commanded Moses. They mounted the onyx stones in gold filigree settings

and engraved them like a seal with the names of the sons of Israel. Then they fastened them on the shoulder pieces of the ephod as memorial stones for the sons of Israel, as the LORD commanded Moses" (Exodus 39:2-7). Think about how the gold, blue, purple and scarlet yarn would stand out against the natural canvas of the tents and the dessert floor. The LORD showed He was Holy in just this way, but of course in *many* other miracles and everyday beauty as well! When we worship God, let's use all the senses He gave us, and give the best for Him. Whether it be cooking, painting, gardening, encouraging, writing, reading, or listening, as long as it's for Him, it can be worship! (Col 3:23)

Gelato al Cioccolato

To make the gelato (Italian for *frozen*) treat, start by deciding to either get an ice cream maker or churn it by hand. The machine that I purchased was very efficient, had a great design, and was about $60. (If you are planning on making ice cream often, it would definitely be a smart investment to get one!) With an ice-cream maker, start by freezing the bowl portion the night before. The process might differ based on the specific machine you have, but that was the case with mine. The next day, combine the milk, cream and 1/2 of the sugar. If you are using nonfat milk, it will still work out great, just heat it a little longer in the second step. Then, you can enunciate the flavors by simmering in a

2 1/2 cups milk

1/3 cup heavy cream

3/4 cup sugar

3 egg yolks

1/2 cup unsweetened, unsalted cocoa powder

1 fine, crumbled dark chocolate bar

saucepan (this is especially helpful when making vanilla or nut ice creams). Cook over high heat. As soon as you start to see the first little air bubbles arising to the top, take it off the heat and set it aside to cool. In a recipe that included this tip, it also said to have a side of milk at hand. By doing so, you can quickly cool any preparations that you think become overly hot. (In fact, this is the recipe that inspired my gelato making the most, and you should check out the cook's tremendous blog. He lived in Italy for some time, so has great advice on authentic Italian cuisine and culture.[a])

While the sugar and milk mixture is cooling, begin to whip the eggs until thickened. Once it has cooled to room temperature, add to the eggs. Mix completely together, then transfer back into the saucepan. Now, you'll heat it all up to cook the eggs and thicken the cream. This second step of the process requires the most patience (you'll also want to add the cocoa powder now). Stirring the whole time, slowly increase the temperature from 'low' to 'medium' to 'high' over 17 minutes! I know this takes a while, but it is very authentic. (Note that it does take less time if you added milk with more fat, or more cream, and

Notes

if more cream, then less milk to average out the balance of cream and milk). I know you can do it! Plus, it's worth it. While you are stirring, you can think of all the wonderful things God has given you over the years, especially in Jesus Christ, who has given you life!!! I'll also include a helpful, little anecdote for you to ponder. When I first made this gelato, I thought that the mixture was not thickening enough (it needs to be, by the way, like a thin soupy milk. When it's ready, take off the heat, and you'll read below what to do next). Anyway, I was heating for 20 minutes, then 30 minutes, all the way to 45 minutes! I finally thought, "Ahah, it's ready," because it was so thick, and I was so tired. However, it was actually too thick! What I had made instead was *pudding*. I know, right? So, here is a bonus recipe for you. When you cook it like this for about 45 minutes, you'll get the most authentic, rich and low-calorie pudding ever! I would recommend eating it with some berries. Praise God for using all things for His good! (Romans 8:28)

Back to the gelato though. When it is soupy, like a thin soupy milk, take it off the heat right away and put into the fridge (the idea is to thicken it *a little*). Refrigerate it for at least 1-2 hours, stirring periodically to prevent a skim from forming. By refrigerating, when you put it back into the ice-cream maker, or use the hand-stirring method, it starts closer to the freezing point and more easily becomes creamy.

After the hour has passed, the fun part begins. If you are using the hand method, begin to stir at every half hour for up to eight hours (sometimes less), until it looks like frozen yogurt. This is what you'll go for. Make sure that it is over an ice-bath and try dry ice to keep the temperature very low (remember to use gloves and caution while handling dry ice!) If you are using an ice-cream maker instead, take the unit out of the freezer and follow the manufacturer's instructions on how to proceed. With mine, you just switch-on the unit and pour the mixture in. After about 20 minutes the texture thickens all the way to a frozen-yogurt-like consistency. Now, you can fold in the crushed chocolate bar, berries or other fruits and eat it as is, or, to make it 'gelatoized,' place it in the freezer for at least another 2 hours. Thaw about 20 minutes before serving and the result will be a thick and creamy gelato! I'd of course recommend serve it with some blueberries, raspberries and blackberries, but I'll leave that to you. Enjoy experimenting with the fine ingredients God has given you, and use it as worship for Him. It is right to give thanks to God! He deserves it!

For more on worship, look at 'Shrimp and Clams,' pg. 94, and footnote 56; listen to the teachings from Door of Hope to follow; and most importantly, read in the Bible! By reading more verses, we can see that God alone is worthy of worship! In His goodness He doesn't need it, but it is so nice, fitting and fun to give Him thanks! He is our LORD and friend; let's read some and thank Him! Psalm 33:1 declares, "Sing joyfully to the LORD, you righteous; it is fitting for the upright to praise him." Psalm 147:1 rejoices, "Praise the LORD. How good it is to sing praises to our God, how pleasant and fitting to praise him!"

White, Josh, narr. "What Is Worship?" Spirit & Truth. Door of Hope, under God's direction, Portland, 16 Aug. 2011. Web. 1 Dec. 2011.
<http://www.doorofhopepdx.org/media/teachings/category/spirit-and-truth.html>.

White, Josh, narr. "Why Should We Sing" Spirit & Truth. Door of Hope, under God's direction, Portland, 16 Aug. 2011. Web. 1 Dec. 2011.
<http://www.doorofhopepdx.org/media/teachings/category/spirit-and-truth.html>.

a. Fariello, Jr., Frank. Memorie di Angelina. Blogspot, July 2010. google. Web. 1 Dec. 2011.
<http://memoriediangelina.blogspot.com/2010/07/gelato-basic-recipe.html>.

90. The data for this potassium table was adopted from the, "Potassium Content of Foods List" on Drugs.com, cited below. The values in milligrams of potassium per serving may vary depending on the specific food and size. Thank God for potassium, and everything that balances our lives! And speaking of fruit, remember, Jesus said, "'I am the vine; you are the branches. If a man remains in me and I in him, he will bear much fruit; apart from me you can do nothing" (John 15:5). Let's remain in Him!

Reuters, Thomson. "Potassium Content Of Foods List." Drugs.com. Drugs.com, 2011. google. Web. 26 Nov. 2011. <http://www.drugs.com/cg/potassium-content-of-foods-list.html>.

91. "God is a gentleman." This insight was given to my pastor, Josh White. It's true. God is a gentleman. Just consider how He loved, loves and will always love us so. Look also at Romans 2:4 about how His kindness leads us to repentance! God is awesome!

For more teachings from Jesus' Word, at Door of Hope, investigate the website below!

"Teachings." Door of Hope. N.p., 2011. Web. 25 Nov. 2011.
<http://www.doorofhopepdx.org/media/teachings.html>.

92. Matthew 5:38-48 says, "'You have heard that it was said, 'Eye for eye, and tooth for tooth.' But I tell you, Do not resist an evil person. If someone strikes you on the right cheek, turn to him the other also. And if someone wants to sue you and take your tunic, let him have your cloak as well. If someone forces you to go one mile, go with him two miles. Give to the one who asks you, and do not turn away from the one who wants to borrow from you. 'You have heard that it was said, 'Love your neighbor and hate your enemy.' But I tell you: Love your enemies and pray for those who persecute you,

that you may be sons of your Father in heaven. He causes his sun to rise on the evil and the good, and sends rain on the righteous and the unrighteous. If you love those who love you, what reward will you get? Are not even the tax collectors doing that? And if you greet only your brothers, what are you doing more than others? Do not even pagans do that? Be perfect, therefore, as your heavenly Father is perfect." (See also footnote 65!)

Also, this Proverb shows that we should be kind to our enemies. By their own convictions they will turn to Christ; we should not burden them. For remember Romans 2:1, which says, "You, therefore, have no excuse, you who pass judgment on someone else, for at whatever point you judge the other, you are condemning yourself, because you who pass judgment do the same things. Now we know that God's judgment against those who do such things is based on truth. So when you, a mere man, pass judgment on them and yet do the same things, do you think you will escape God's judgment? Or do you show contempt for the riches of his kindness, tolerance and patience, not realizing that God's kindness leads you toward repentance?" It is God's kindness that leads us to repentance! Therefore, let's be kind to everyone, including our 'enemies,' so that they can be turned into friends when they hear about God, the Holy Spirit and what Jesus did for them!!! We have to tell them about Jesus though (Mt 28:19-20)!

a. The historical information about Proverbs 25:22 was noted in my Bible commentary on Romans 12:20, where Paul exemplifies this verse: "'The most important one,' answered Jesus, 'is this: 'Hear, O Israel, the Lord our God, the Lord is one. Love the Lord your God with all your heart and with all your soul and with all your mind and with all your strength.' The second is this: 'Love your neighbor as yourself.' There is no commandment greater than these'" (Mark 12:29-31). The idea of turning one's cheek is seen throughout Scripture such as in the greatest two commandments! Praise God!

See the commentary on Romans 12:20, pg. 2051
Life Application Bible: New International Version. Wheaton And Grand Rapids: Tyndale House Publishers, Inc. and Zondervan, 1991. 2051. Print.

93. The information for the pasta table was compiled from several sources listed below. No matter what shape or size you are, God made you and you are beautiful! Of course, we can be healthy and exercise, but there is no need to worry (Matthew 6:25-34). Jesus is what matters! Let's fix our eyes on Him! (Hebrews 12:1-29)

a. "Different types of pasta: an A-Z guide." Pasta Recipes Made Easy. Pasta Recipes Made Easy, n.d.

google. Web. 10 Dec. 2011. <http://www.pasta-recipes-made-easy.com/different-types-of-pasta.html>.
b. "Pasta." Brooklyn Pizza Works and Italian Restaurant. Brooklyn Pizza Works, n.d. google. Web. 10
Dec. 2011. <http://www.brooklyn-pizza-works.com/pasta.htm>.
c. "Couscous." Collins English Dictionary - Complete & Unabridged 10th Edition. HarperCollins Publishers. 09 Dec. 2011. <Dictionary.com http://dictionary.reference.com/browse/couscous>.
d. "Pasta Shapes." National Pasta Association. Kellen Company, n.d. google. Web. 10 Dec. 2011.
<http://www.ilovepasta.org/shapes.html>.

94. For the Bible citations in this book, there are two sources: the 'Life Application Bible,'[a] given to me as a
gift from a true sister and friend in Christ, Carol Steele; and 'Blue Letter Bible,'[b] an online organization
that locates verses with various searches. Check them out and may God continue to lead us in His
Word. Let's pray and ask Him to join us when reading so He can teach us through the Holy Spirit what
He has for us every day! (Hebrews 4:12; Romans 8:26: John 1:1) [†]Also, the Biblical measurements, on
the inside cover, were adopted from the, 'Table of Weights and Measures' in the Life Application Bible.

a. Life Application Bible: New International Version. Wheaton And Grand Rapids: Tyndale House
Publishers, Inc. and Zondervan, 1991. 1054-55 and 2337, respectively. Print.
b. Blue Letter Bible. Blue Letter Bible, n.d. Web. 3 Oct. 2011. <http://www.blueletterbible.org/>.

95. Here is a great footnote! For more teachings from Jesus' Word, at Door of Hope, investigate the
website below!

> "Teachings." Door of Hope. N.p., 2011. Web. 25 Nov. 2011.
> <http://www.doorofhopepdx.org/media/teachings.html>.

Well, I didn't get to footnote 100, but it was close! Thanks for reading some footnotes. I
know that God will continue to bless you. And in all we do, may we remember the first and
greatest commandment. As recorded in Mark 12:29-31, "'The most important one,' answered
Jesus, 'is this: 'Hear, O Israel, the Lord our God, the Lord is one. Love the Lord your God with
all your heart and with all your soul and with all your mind and with all your strength.' The
second is this: 'Love your neighbor as yourself.' There is no commandment greater than these.'"

thirsty" (John 6:35). Let's come to Jesus and His Word, which gives us daily sustenance. Without Him, we will die! Let's let Him and His eternal life live in us and love Him and others more! The greatest commandment is is to, "'Love the Lord your God with all your heart and with all your soul and with all your mind.' This is the first and greatest commandment. And the second is like it: 'Love your neighbor as yourself.' All the Law and the Prophets hang on these two command ments'" (Matthew 22:37-39). It's really all about God and His love for us; He loved us so much, in fact, that *He died for us!* He is our God! (John 3:16-17), 25, 132, 219, 221

Church
   Church is not a building. We are all part of the Church body, like the wife, and Jesus is the Husband (Ephesians 5:29-32)!

Christ
   Jesus Christ is the 'Messiah' (in Greek) and 'Anointed One' (in Hebrew). He is the long-awaited Savior (Jesus means *the LORD saves*), God's Son, as God in the flesh, to set us free from our sins! He's definitely worth waiting for! It is true that, "Therefore,

there is now no condemnation for those who are in Christ Jesus, because through Christ Jesus the law of the Spirit of life set me free from the law of sin and death" (Romans 8:1-2). Jesus Christ sets us free! Praise Him!!!

clean, 10, 21, 45, 108, 147, 156, 166, 173, 176, 214, *thanks to Jesus!* (Revelation 7:14)

coffee: another gift from God!

Coffee is great because it has antioxidants, but it does raise your blood pressure. 131

commandments, 111, 132, 134, 137, 167, 210

communion, 25

community, 78, 101

cornerstone, 123

Counselor

Another Name for the Holy Spirit, Jesus uses this Name in John 14:16, 26; 15:26; and 16:7 (see footnote 47). 80, 113, 144, 161, 163

Couscous, 52

creation, 47, 56, 101, 126, 154

creativity, 30, 41, 74, 124, 134, 149, 151, 217, 219

Creator, 47

crevettes

French for *shrimp*, 48, 86

cross, 10, 15, 17, 25, 33, 42, 48, 68, 121, 126, 131, 138, 139, 146, 148, 152, 156, 173, 175, 176

crucified, 25, 128, 141, 170

crust, 103, 114, 155, 173, 174, 175

cupcakes, 123

D

daily bread

Jesus is our daily bread. John records, "Then Jesus declared, 'I am the bread of life. He who comes to me will never go hungry, and he who believes in me will never be thirsty" (John 6:35). 26

dairy, 17, 45, 219

dairy-free, 45

day, 1, 9, 15, 17, 25, 29, 30, 33, 35, 45, 56, 59, 68, 74, 77, 78, 86, 89, 94, 101, 103, 104, 107, 111, 124, 128, 132, 134, 139, 140, 141, 149, 153, 158, 167, 169, 176, 210, 220, 221

dedication, 41

deep, 162, 165

Design, 4

Desserts, 5, 118, 121, 126

disciple

A follower of Jesus Christ! 6, 15, 25, 26, 30, 45, 80, 85, 126, 141, 145, 160, 162, 163, 166, 169, 172, 173, 176

do not doubt, 152, 153

Dolci, 118

Door of Hope

The Church I go to in Portland. Here is the website address for the teachings: http://www.doorofhopepdx.org/media/teachings.html. The name also appears in Hosea 2:15! 136, 137, 139, 155, 164, 171, 172, 176, 178, 179, 221

double colander, 93, 148, 149, 150

ship? You were made to be completed in God! He is for you and you are for Him. Are you for Him? Let's all live by receiving Him and our lives will have Truth! (See also footnote 45.), 33, 42, 52, 68, 72, 104, 114, 126, 142, 149, 151, 153, 157, 161, 166, 176

Religion: true *religion* from God

"Religion that God our Father accepts as pure and faultless is this: to look after orphans and widows in their distress and to keep oneself from being polluted by the world" (James 1:27). Jesus is not about being religious. Look at the Gospel accounts. Religion doesn't save us, He saves us! He instead wants us to be freed through His amazing love! He really is all about the greatest commandment of love, "Jesus replied: 'Love the Lord your God with all your heart and with all your soul and with all your mind.' This is the first and greatest commandment. And the second is like it: 'Love your neighbor as yourself.' All the Law and the Prophets hang on these two commandments'" (Matthew 22:37-40). (See also footnote 37.), 137, 151, 164

repent

Repent literally means, *change directions*. It takes us humbling ourselves before God and realizing our mistakes. Then, let's ask God to forgive us, change direction and He is right there waiting! All the time. We don't need to repent by rote over and over again though. That is really missing the point. Instead, by fixing our eyes on Jesus, it changes our whole heart and mindset! Hebrews 12:2-3 says, "Let us fix our eyes on Jesus, the author and perfecter of our faith, who for the joy set before him endured the cross, scorning its shame, and sat down at the right hand of the throne of God. Consider him who endured such opposition from sinful men, so that you will not grow weary and lose heart." 161

repentance, 21, 126, 128, 161, 167, 171, 216

rest

In Jesus we find true rest, or Shalom. 33, 42, 45, 56, 77, 89, 93, 94, 103, 107, 116, 124, 140, 141, 150, 157, 171

rhubarb, 124, 174, 175

righteous, 15, 74, 113, 114, 138, 142, 151, 154, 155, 157, 161, 171, 178

righteousness, 17, 51, 73, 86, 116, 123, 132, 157, 167, 180

risen, 15, 25, 47, 77, 141, 148, 160

rock

Jesus is our big rock. Jesus calls Peter, *Petros* (which means *little rock*), because Peter has faith in Him as the Christ come to save. If we have faith in Jesus and put what He is saying into practice, nothing can shake us because nothing is greater than Him! Matthew records Jesus saying, "Therefore everyone who hears these words of mine and puts them into practice is like a wise man who built his house on the rock. The rain came down, the streams rose, and the winds blew and beat against that house; yet it did not fall, because it had its foundation on the rock. But everyone who hears these words of mine and does not put them into practice is like a foolish man who built his house on sand. The rain came down, the streams rose, and the winds blew and beat against that house, and it fell with a great crash" (Matthew 7:24-27). 153

S

Sabbath

The Sabbath was made for a day of rest. It is a gift, like everything we have, from God (Mark 2:27). It is not to be a religious ritual though. For God would like us to heal and love Him especially on these days that are set apart, or *Holy*, from the others. It gives us time to love Him and others better. Matthew records Jesus healing a person on the Sabbath: "How much more valuable is a man than a sheep! Therefore it is lawful to do good on the Sabbath. Then he said to the man, 'Stretch out your hand.' So he stretched it out and it was completely restored, just as sound as the other" (Matthew 12:13). Let's use the Sabbaths God gives us to really do good for Him, only in Him and in His direction! John 15:5 says,"I am the vine; you are the branches. If a man remains in me and I in him, he will bear much fruit; apart from me you can do nothing." (See also Matthew 25:31-46.), 77, 78, 145

sacrifice

Jesus was the sacrifice for our sins. We now don't have to be religious or whatever to earn it. We cannot earn it. Jesus is the Way, the Truth and the Life (John 14:6). In Him we have this Life. Praise God for being so humble and loving to send His Son to die for us, so that we could have a right relationship with Him! This is incredibly amazing. This is His offer to us. Let's gladly receive it with joy and tell others! 10, 15, 45, 52, 60, 68, 78, 114, 131, 142, 144, 156, 163, 169

salt

Jesus says to His disciples, or *followers* (which can be us too), "You are the salt of the earth.

But if the salt loses its saltiness, how can it be made salty again? It is no longer good for anything, except to be thrown out and trampled by men" (Matthew 5:13). Even if we don't eat a lot of salt, we can be salty in Christ. The Holy Spirit in us is what gives us the flavor of His love in our society. It is not by our own efforts, though. Jesus doesn't say, 'Be the salt of the earth.' He says, "You are the salt of the earth." In Christ we are a new creation and He lives in us! He gives us a new heart and loves people through us! Let's invite Him in and let Him do so! (2 Corinthians 5:17; Ezekiel 11:19; 36:26; 1 Corinthians 6:19), 6, 9, 19, 41, 60, 63, 64, 72, 73, 77, 80, 103, 104, 107, 116, 121, 131,134, 139, 153, 155, 168, 212, 218, 219

salvation

Jesus is the way for our salvation! There is no other way, which is a good thing, because it is so hard! Jesus died and then rose to life again to defeat the consequence of sin, being death, so that we can be with God! Romans 6:23 says, "For the wages of sin is death, but the gift of God is eternal life in Christ Jesus our Lord." And John 14:6 says, "Jesus answered, 'I am the way and the truth and the life. No one comes to the Father except through me." By remaining in Him, we have eternal life!!! Consider, too, John 15:4, when Jesus uses the metaphor of a vine. He

tells us, "Remain in me, and I will remain in you. No branch can bear fruit by itself; it must remain in the vine. Neither can you bear fruit unless you remain in me." Let's remain in Him! 17, 86, 139, 143, 162

saturated, 10, 21, 48, 138, 155, 218

sauce, 15, 71, 73, 90, 111, 114, 116, 124, 158, 170, 171, 219

save, 25, 35, 56, 59, 111, 126, 137, 140, 143, 146, 148, 151, 157, 159, 160, 161, 162, 164, 168, 171, 172

saved, 108, 157, 161, 162

Savior, 144, 160, 161, 163

Scripture, 6, 48, 86, 121, 123, 131, 132, 154, 155, 157, 161, 162, 163, 165, 167, 168, 170, 173, 210, 211

seafood, 15, 48, 74, 93, 94, 149, 150

seek

Jesus says, "Ask and it will be given to you; seek and you will find; knock and the door will be opened to you. For everyone who asks receives; he who seeks finds; and to him who knocks, the door will be opened" (Matthew 7:7-8). When we ask for something from Jesus for Jesus then He grants it - like if we ask for the Holy Spirit in us! James reminds us though, "When you ask, you do not receive, because you ask with wrong motives, that you may spend what you get on your pleasures" (James 4:3). Let's ask for things in Jesus' Name! (See also

from the Father, full of grace and truth. John testifies concerning him. He cries out, saying, 'This was he of whom I said, 'He who comes after me has surpassed me because he was before me.' From the fullness of his grace we have all received one blessing after another. For the law was given through Moses; grace and truth came through Jesus Christ. No one has ever seen God, but God the One and Only, who is at the Father's side, has made him known." Jesus is the way, the truth and the life (John 14:6), and He saved us from our sins so that we could be with God in right relationship! Also, in the Old Testament's culture, the firstborn son would get all of the inheritance and blessing. Now, we get it because we have all become sons through faith in Christ Jesus. It is really a term referring to receiving His blessing!!! This is good news! Galatians 3:26-29 says, "You are all sons of God through faith in Christ Jesus, for all of you who were baptized into Christ have clothed yourselves with Christ. There is neither Jew nor Greek, slave nor free, male nor female, for you are all one in Christ Jesus. If you belong to Christ, then you are Abraham's seed, and heirs according to the promise." So whoever we are, whatever race, or culture, anything, if we have faith in Jesus, the One and Only Son, then we become co-heirs with Him and He saves us;

He is the way (John 14:6), and we get the gift! This is good news indeed! Thanks be to God!!! Romans 8:17 says, "Now if we are children, then we are heirs - heirs of God and co-heirs with Christ, if indeed we share in his sufferings in order that we may also share in his glory." Let's invite Him in and remain in Him no matter the small cost. Amen (Amen means *Let it be so*)! I mean think of the price He paid! He died for us so that we could be right with the Father! He is the One and Only God and He is the One and Only Son! He is Jesus, our Savior! (See also footnote 47, 'Jesus,' 'God' and 'Holy Spirit.'), 25, 42, 47, 52, 60, 80, 107, 114, 126, 131, 143, 144, 145, 147, 148, 149, 151, 154, 161, 162, 166, 169, 176

song

Let's enter God's courts and presence with thanksgiving, sometimes through song: "Enter his gates with thanksgiving and his courts with praise; give thanks to him and praise his name" (Psalm 100:4; this is my favorite Psalm. What is yours?). Both the start and end of this book give thanks to God because God deserves it! How fun it is to sing praises to God! He is the One who saves us! 1, 17, 25, 41, 94, 151, 154, 169, 173, 179, 210, 211

Sopas, 54

soup, 5, 15, 51, 54, 56, 60, 63, 64, 77, 139, 140, 141, 150, 219

sword

We are told in Scripture that, "For the word of God is living and active. Sharper than any double-edged sword, it penetrates even to dividing soul and spirit, joints and marrow; it judges the thoughts and attitudes of the heart" (Hebrews 4:12). Let's daily read the Word of God and ask for God's Holy Spirit to be in us. Only because He has defeated sin and death can we share in life with Him, with Him in us! (1 Cor 6:19-20), 17, 132, 214

T

tapenad

A tapenad is an olive-based spread. Olives are really yummy, but should be avoided with a low sodium diet! It's ok, Jesus loves you so much. He died for your sins and sets you free! Hallelujah! 35

taste, 124, 175

teaching, 41, 51, 52, 80, 86, 108, 116, 123, 126, 132, 139, 145, 153, 162, 166, 167, 176, 210

tell, 9, 15, 25, 72, 86, 114, 139, 141, 143, 144, 152, 153, 154, 155, 156, 163, 165, 171, 176

temple

We are told in 1 Corinthians, "Do you not know that your body is a temple of the Holy Spirit, who is in you, whom you have received from God? You are not your own; you were bought at a price. Therefore honor God with your body" (1 Corinthians 6:19-20). The Holy Spirit can live in us! Let's invite Him in and honor Him with all of us! (See also 'His Spirit,' 'Holy Spirit,' and 'Spirit.'), 80, 113, 142, 158, 214, 215, 218

Ten Commandments, 131

testament, 85, 126, 160

thanks, 1, 25, 30, 35, 41, 42, 59, 60, 63, 68, 94, 103, 104, 124, 131, 140, 142, 147, 149, 151, 152, 154, 162, 172, 175, 178, 179, 214, 221

thanksgiving, 1, 41, 59, 78

the Anointed One: Christ!

'The Anointed One' is Jesus! He came to save people from sin and it's oppression, so that we can be freed and with God in Holy matrimony, or right relationship (see 'Church', 'Husband,' and 'wife'). Sometimes Jesus is referred to as the Christ (Greek), or Messiah (Hebrew). Many people were expecting Him to come because of prophecy about Him. Jesus filled all prophecy, which something only the Savior God could do, but people didn't expect that it would be Him. They were at first looking for a military or political leader to relieve them from the oppression of *Rome*. What Jesus did though was much greater, far greater! In Daniel we read, "He was given authority, glory and sovereign power; all peoples, nations and men of every language worshiped him. His dominion is an everlasting dominion that will not pass away, and his kingdom is one that will never be destroyed" (Daniel 7:14). His Kingdom is an everlasting Kingdom that is based on Him, in peace, love and truth. He set us free from sin and death! Let's live and trust in Him forever! Amen! 160

the way and the truth and the life

Jesus and only Jesus is the way and the truth and the life. It is written, "Jesus answered, 'I am the way and the truth and the life. No one comes to the Father except through me. If you really knew me, you would know my Father as well. From now on, you do know him and have seen him" (John 14:6-7). Jesus died on the cross for our sins and took our punishment, so that we could have a right relationship with the Father! God did this for us! We cannot come to God any other way, like by our own deeds. The only way is Jesus! If you are trying to on your own and frustrated, or tying to follow all the rules, it's impossible! Jesus did the impossible thing, though, and He raised to life, defeating death and sin in our lives forever! This is Good News because there is no other way. In Mark we read, "Jesus looked at them and said, 'With man this is impossible, but not with God; all things are possible with God'" (Mark 10:27). Let's rejoice and trust in Him! Let's put our whole lives into knowing Him,

because our lives are dependant on Him. 15, 107, 113, 114, 128, 150, 154, 156, 160, 162, 164, 166, 167, 171, 174, 178

thirst: (See Jesus' Word in Jn 7:38, and Jn 6:35.) Jesus said, "Blessed are those who hunger and thirst for righteousness, for they will be filled" (Matthew 5:6). It is one of the Beatitudes, or character traits of God and His kingdom! Look them all up in Matthew 5:1-12! 25, 48, 132, 154, 155, 165, 216

Tips section, 210

treats, 94, 96, 121

Trinity: Holy Trinity

The Trinity is not something made up! God is the Father, Jesus is the Son, our Savior, who is still God, and there is the Holy Spirit from God. They are One God, who is our God! God, our heavenly Father, humbled Himself and entered humanity through His Son, who died for our sins. He loved us so much that He died for us!!! And now we all have access to Him through the Holy Spirit! This is amazing! To read of God's Three-In-One nature, look to: Exodus 3:14, when God declares His Name; John 1:1-2, 14; 14:10; 14:11; Matthew 28:19-20, with the Name being singular; and footnote 47! 42, 72, 138, 145, 161

trust, 10, 25, 30, 35, 47, 48, 59, 68, 71, 94, 101, 104, 123, 124, 140, 143, 145, 147, 159, 172, 173

Wonderful Counselor

A Name for God! He is our Wonderful Counselor indeed. See the above entry and consider that God has given us His Holy Spirit, another name for 'Counselor,' to guide us continually! He can be in us: God in us, leading us by His Holy Spirit! All we have to do is receive Him and trust in Him! (See also the verses were Jesus talks about sending the Holy Spirit in John 14:16, 26; 15:26; 16:17; and read footnote 47.), 144

Word

Jesus is the Word in the flesh! John 1:1 says, "In the beginning was the Word, and the Word was with God, and the Word was God. He was with God in the beginning." The Word is God, and always has been! And In John 1:14, we learn that, "The Word became flesh and made his dwelling among us. We have seen his glory, the glory of the One and Only, who came from the Father, full of grace and truth." Thus, Jesus is the Word in the flesh! He is fully God, and also fully human, so He can save us from our sins! He bridges the gap between sinful man and a perfectly good, loving God. We read about Jesus' amazing work of bringing us into a right relationship with God in Ephe-sians 2:14-18, which says, "For he himself is our peace, who has made the two one and has destroyed the barrier, the dividing wall of hostility, by abolishing in his flesh the law with its commandments and regulations. His purpose was to create in himself one new man out of the two, thus making peace, and in this one body to reconcile both of them to God through the cross, by which he put to death their hostility. He came and preached peace to you who were far away and peace to those who were near. For through him we both have access to the Father by one Spirit." Jesus really is the way! There is no other! We read about this in John 14:6, when Jesus says, "'I am the way and the truth and the life. No one comes to the Father except through me." Thank God for sending His One and Only Son to die for us so that we can be right with Him all the time, with His Holy Spirit in us (1 Corinthians 6:19)! He really does love all of us so much!

There are so many more amazing truths about God, just like these, that Jesus (*the Word*) daily reveals to us. Consider what is said in John 20:31 and 21:25! We should *read* God's Word every opportunity we get to be with Him and rejoice in His love (see 'Jesus' Word,' 132). And, the Holy Spirit also daily reveals His truth to us, so we should *listen* for His guidance. We will see that He is

God, He is our daily bread, and without Him, we will die. We need His sustenance desperately, for we are made to be in a right relationship with Him, and as a result, others! Hallelujah for Him providing the way and the truth and the life! (See also (1) the greatest commandment, which is as, "Jesus replied: 'Love the Lord your God with all your heart and with all your soul and with all your mind.' This is the first and greatest commandment. And the second is like it: 'Love your neighbor as yourself.' All the Law and the Prophets hang on these two commandments'" (Matthew 22:37-40).; (2) Hebrews 4:12; (3) 'sword'; and (4) 'daily bread').), 12, 17, 25, 26, 30, 33, 51, 64, 74, 86, 93, 113, 123, 126, 132, 146, 148, 154, 161, 166, 167, 170, 172, 173, 221
work
   "Jesus answered, 'The work of God is this: to believe in the one he has sent'" (John 6:29). 9, 30, 33, 35, 41, 47, 56, 59, 68, 74, 77, 80, 86, 93, 95, 123, 124, 126, 132, 141, 142, 148, 149, 151, 152, 156, 158, 159, 160, 164, 167, 171, 174, 176, 177, 210, 219
working together, 42, 93, 149, 157
world, 6, 25, 47, 52, 59, 103, 107, 126, 137, 149, 151, 154, 158, 162, 164, 165, 169, 176, 211
worry
   Jesus teaches us not to worry! Consider if we have *Jesus*, the One who *truly loves us*

and has *died for our sins* so that we can be *united with God* in a right relationship, because He loves us so much, why should we worry? Jesus also reminds us, as recorded in Matthew, "Therefore I tell you, do not worry about your life, what you will eat or drink; or about your body, what you will wear. Is not life more important than food, and the body more important than clothes. Look at the birds of the air; they do not sow or reap or store away in barns, and yet your heavenly Father feeds them. Are you not much more valuable than they? Who of you by worrying can add a single hour to his life?" (Matthew 6:25-27; try reading the rest as well). Jesus did it! Our response should naturally be to trust in Him. Let's let Him work in us, and let's praise Him for taking care of all our needs all the time! Really, He is always there, and always for us! Romans 8:31, says, "What, then, shall we say in response to this? If God is for us, who can be against us?" God has everything under control! Let's remain in Him and receive His Holy Spirit! Jesus reminds, "Remain in me, and I will remain in you. No branch can bear fruit by itself; it must remain in the vine. Neither can you bear fruit unless you remain in me" (John 15:4). Amen and Hallelujah for Jesus providing the way! 9, 30, 56, 68, 165, 187, 188

worship (See the first commandment: Exd 20:3)
Worship is so cool! We get to thank God for
what He has done! And many things can be
done in thanks to God! We usually sing
when we go to Church and this is beautiful,
but there are other senses aside from
hearing. If you are gardening, then garden
for Him! You can say thanks for all of the
wonderful plants and foods He has given us.
They are so strong and yet delicate (Romans
8:1). Or, if you are a teacher, then teach for
Him! Jesus loves how children receive Him
with joy and are not weighed down by the
weight of the world. They just trust (Matthew
19:14; Mark 10:14; Luke 18:16). There is
so much that He has for us! Let's worship Him!

Also, let's remember God deserves our
worship! He is God and He is good. He
loves us so much and has done so much for
us! He is perfect. He even sent His Son to
die for us so that we could be set free from
sin and separation from *right relationship*. All
we have to do is receive Him by having faith
in Him! This is amazing! He is amazing. I'd
say that worship, then, is partially there to
realize how good He is! It's fun, an honor,
and fitting to praise Him (Psalm 147:1). It is
yet another gift that God gives us! Let's talk
to Him and tell Him thanks!

In Leviticus, Exodus and Numbers, there
are many accounts of God telling His people

how to worship. The heart of these messages
apply to us today. All of the senses are
involved. There is woodcarving, building,
sewing, tent-making, incense-burning,
food-preparation, singing, dancing, talking
with Him; everything and anything. God
shows us that He deserves the best and we
get to hang out with Him, our God!!! Wow,
Praise God! (Plus, a beautiful side note is
that after writing this section, God really put
it on my heart to learn more about worship.
Well, guess what the new series was on at
Door of Hope just the past few weeks?
Worship! God is good!!! You can hear the
inspired teachings at: http://www.doorofhope
pdx.org/media/teachings/category/spirit-
truth.html. See also 41, 137, and Matthew
22:37-40!), 1, 41, 131, 137, 151, 152, 179, 211

Priase the LORD!!!
"Let everything that has breath praise the
LORD. Praise the LORD" (Psalm 150:6).

On the following pages, you can Praise the
LORD for what He has done in your life!
Maybe take your own notes about what He is
telling you; it can be on cooking or anything.
Draw, paint, whatever you think He is leading
you in. *Let* Him join you!!! He has already
offered to join us by sending His Son Jesus and
His Holy Spirit! He is always right there! He is
so good and He loves us! He is God!

Praise the LORD!!!

Thanks be to God!!!

Here are some tips that will hopefully help your culinary and life experience. The tips are written in smaller poetic statements so you can learn many lessons from them. In the Bible, too, there are some whole books written this way. Psalms is a beautifully poetic book, written with amazing songs and poems to God. Proverbs has short wisdom sayings and offers insights into God (some ideas are paralleled, some are contrasted, and some are one-liners). Ecclesiastes has longer, but still concise, life lessons about living for God. So with each tip here, there is a following 'tip,' or verse, of great wisdom that is influenced by Him from these three books. For example, "All the recipe is helpful. If you read it through to start, when you begin, you will know where you're going."; "All Scripture is God-breathed and is useful for teaching, rebuking, correcting and training in right-eousness, so that the man of God may be thoroughly equipped for every good work" (2 Timothy 3:16; which isn't a part of the three, but was so relevant!) It is fitting that these tips go along with Scripture, because God has so much for us in *all* parts of the Bible (2 Timothy 3:16)! Hallelujah!

For each Scriptural 'tip,' you can learn connections and wisdom from Him, for Him, the only wisdom that really matters! For James writes, "But the wisdom that comes from heaven is first of all pure; then peace-loving, considerate, submissive, full of mercy and good fruit, impartial and sincere. Peacemakers who sow in peace raise a harvest of righteousness." Luke also records Jesus saying, "If you then, though you are evil, know how to give good gifts to your children, how much more will your Father in heaven give the Holy Spirit to those who ask him!" When we're reading the Bible, or doing anything, let's ask for God to give us His Holy Spirit and teach what He wants for us that day! Also, let's pray He helps us live out that lesson in loving Him and others better! For the great-est commandments are to, "Love the Lord your God with all your heart and with all your soul and with all your mind and with all your strength.' The second is this: 'Love your neighbor as yourself.' There is no commandment greater than these" (Mark 12:30). He will answer these prayers! (Matthew 7:7; Luke 11:9; James 1:5, and read James 4:3-10†)

†Jesus wants our hearts to be for Him! He gives us freedom in Him to share with others, not to live for ourselves. Paul reminds the Galatians that, "You, my brothers, were called to be free. But do not use your freedom to indulge the sinful nature; rather, serve one another in love" (Galatians 5:13). Therefore, we should also pray and ask God for His will, not our own desires. Jesus says to us, "Ask and it will be given to you: seek and you will find; knock and the door will be opened to you. For everyone who asks receives;

he who seeks finds; and to him who knocks, the door will be opened" (Matthew 7:7) But James reminds us that sometimes, "When you ask, you do not receive, because you ask with wrong motives, that you may spend what you get on your pleasures. You adulterous people, don't you know that friendship with the world is hatred toward God? Anyone who chooses to be a friend of the world becomes an enemy of God. Or do you think Scripture says without reason that the spirit he caused to live in us envies intensely? But he gives us more grace. That is why Scripture says: 'God opposes the proud but gives grace to the humble.' Submit yourselves, then, to God. Resist the devil, and he will flee from you. Come near to God and he will come near to you. Wash your hands, you sinners, and purify your hearts, you double-minded. Grieve, mourn and wail. Change your laughter to mourning and your joy to gloom. Humble yourselves before the Lord, and he will lift you up" (James 4:3-10).

1. Shout for joy to the LORD for all the wonderful ingredients He has given to you!

> "Shout for joy to the LORD, all the earth. Worship the LORD with gladness; come before him with joyful songs. Know that the LORD is God. It is he who made us, and we are his, we are his people, the sheep of his pasture" (Psalm 100:1-3).

2. If your knife is dull, then use a bread knife to cut tomatoes.

> "If the ax is dull and its edge unsharpened, more strength is needed but skill will bring success" (Ecclesiastes 10:10).

3. Before the cooking even starts, it is better to have a preparation bowl for each ingredient; to cut, mince, and dice everything prior, than to have to peel and cut the garlic after the chicken is ready. (Truly, try to get all the ingredients ready at the beginning!) . . .

.... (continued)

"You prepare a table before me in the presence of my enemies. You anoint my head with oil; my cup overflows. Surely goodness and love will follow me all the days of my life, and I will dwell in the house of the LORD forever" (Psalm 23:5-6).

4. There are amounts of ingredients that may seem right, but it is better to pray and ask God to lead you in everything, including cooking. Practice receiving His Presence, and have Him help you even cook.

   "There is a way that seems right to a man, but in the end it leads to death" (Proverbs 14:12).

5. Adding garlic and onions at the end will prevent them from becoming too charred.

   "For this God is our God for ever and ever; he will be our guide even to the end" (Psalm 48:14).

6. When making a meal, consider if there are people who do not like spice as much or if there are some people with salt, dairy, gluten, vegan, vegetarian, or soy diets. It will be better to have everyone loved.

   "That everyone may eat and drink, and find satisfaction in all his toil - this is the gift of God" (Ecclesiastes 3:13).

7. Unwatched broiled bread does burn and a watched pot is very patient.

   "My soul waits for the Lord more than watchmen wait for the

morning, more than watchmen wait for the morning"
(Psalm 130:6).

8. The dinner plans of one who is loving towards their guests in Christ is better than someone who focuses on the meal or decor instead.

> "The plans of the diligent lead to profit as surely as haste leads to poverty" (Proverbs 21:5).

9. Boiling a chicken for soup without a vegetable strainer on the bottom, or something to prevent the chicken from burning, is like a burnt skunk.

> "Like a madman shooting firebrands or deadly arrows is a man who deceives his neighbor and says, 'I was only joking'" (Proverbs 26:18-19)!

10. Saving some green for garnish, or extra ingredients, will leave you and your guests bowing down to the LORD.

> "The LORD is God, and he has made his light shine upon us. With boughs in hand, join in the festal procession up to the horns of the altar" (Psalm 118:27).

11. Cooking with plastic or putting it in the dishwasher is not the right place for it.

> "There is a time for everything, and a season for every activity under heaven: a time to be born and a time to die, a time to plant and a time to uproot, a time to kill and a time to heal, a time to tear down and a time to build, a time to weep and a time to laugh, a time to mourn and a time to dance, a time to

scatter stones and a time to gather them, a time to embrace and a time to refrain, a time to search and a time to give up, a time to keep and a time to throw away, a time to tear and a time to mend, a time to be silent and a time to speak, a time to love and a time to hate, a time for war and a time for peace" (Ecclesiastes 3:1-8).

12. When cutting a cake, it is very nice to use a hot, clean knife.

"Reckless words pierce like a sword, but the tongue of the wise brings healing" (Proverbs 12:18).

13. Thank God for what He has given you, food and everything. All good we have is from Him!

"Blessed are those you choose and bring near to live in your courts! We are filled with the good things of your house, of your holy temple" (Psalm 65:4).

14. Cooking in a rush will surely give you dryness, but waiting for the LORD and something to steam brings perfection.

"Wait for the LORD; be strong and take heart and wait for the LORD" (Psalm 27:14).

15. Cooking on high heat starts off the meal with a sear. Lowering the temperature later helps to make it tender.

"When I was a boy in my father's house, still tender, and an only child of my mother, he taught me and said, 'Lay hold of my words with all your heart; keep my commands and you will live. Get wisdom, get understanding; do not forget my words or swerve from them" (Proverbs 4:3-5; try reading the rest.) (I just opened my Bible straight to this one, without looking for a verse with 'tender' in it - I know God wanted us to see it and stay pure!)

16. Steaming red onions for too long will remove their color, so add red onions at the end.

"One thing I ask of the LORD, this is what I seek: that I may dwell in the house of the LORD all the days of my life, to gaze upon the beauty of the LORD and to seek him in his temple" (Psalm 27:4).

17. Likewise, cooking or baking basil will leave you with a bad color and no taste. Add the basil at the end.

"Charm is deceptive, and beauty is fleeting; but a woman who fears the LORD is to be praised" (Proverbs 31:30).

18. Proportions are only suggestions. In faith, Jesus will satisfy us and provide us with more than we need. (Look at Luke 9:10-17.)

"My flesh and my heart may fail, but God is the strength of my heart and my portion forever" (Psalm 73:26).

19. Old bread makes new bruschetta.

"Remember, O LORD, your great mercy and love, for they are from of old. Remember not the sins of my youth and my rebe-lious ways; according to your love remember me, for you are good, O LORD. Good and upright is the LORD; therefore he instructs sinners in his ways. He guides the humble in what is right and teaches them his way. All the ways of the LORD are loving

and faithful for those who keep the demands of his covenant" (Psalm 25:10).

20. Shrimp cook fast; if they are taking too long, then turn up the heat. Chicken likes to be steamed and steak loves to marinate.

"If your enemy is hungry, give him food to eat; if he is thirsty, give him water to drink. In doing this, you will heap burning coals on his head, and the LORD will reward you" (Proverbs 25:22).†

21. Don't forget the healthy snack of popcorn! By making it on a stove, with just some olive oil, let it steam with a cover.

"Smoke rose from his nostrils; consuming fire came from his mouth, burning coals blazed out of it" (Psalm 18:8).

22. Chopping garlic and onions beforehand, along with all other ingredients, is a smart idea. When you have left-over ingredients, store them in the fridge for next time. Always ask those you are living with though, if they can live with the smell.

"As dead flies give perfume a bad smell, so a little folly outweighs wisdom and honor" (Ecclesiastes 10:1).

† Some proverbs seem to not make sense or go together. However, there is still a lesson there. In this proverb, we learn as Jesus said, "So in everything, do to others what you would have them do to you, for this sums up the Law and the Prophets" (Matthew 7:12). Certain things need certain conditions. In the time this proverb was written, "This may refer to an Egyptian tradition of carrying a pan of burning charcoal on one's head as a public act of repentance." Thus, enemies will be convicted by their actions and only Christ can change their hearts (see Mat 5:38-48.)†92a

23. Don't worry in general! Also, don't worry if you only have water and vegetables with the LORD. (Look at Luke 12:25-34.)

"Better a meal of vegetables where there is love than a fattened calf with hatred" (Proverbs 15:17).

24. Enjoying wine and olive oil with a meal is one thing. Living for them is another.

"He who loves pleasure will become poor; whoever loves wine and oil will never be rich" (Proverbs 21:17).

25. Try a different selection of nuts or cheeses, toppings and other ingredients. Be refreshed by Him and His creativity. But remember, we are for Him who endures forever; everything else is meaningless.

"However many years a man may live, let him enjoy them all. But let him remember the days of darkness, for they will be many. Everything to come is meaningless" (Ecclesiastes 11:8).

26. Making food is like making art, which is like listening to God.

"Stop listening to instruction, my son, and you will stray from the words of knowledge" (Proverbs 19:27).

27. "Let everything that has breath praise the LORD. Praise the LORD" (Psalm 150:6, the last Psalm).

"Let everything that has breath praise the Lord. Praise the LORD" (Psalm 150:6).

Praise the LORD!!!

Foods to Avoid

There are certain foods that we should all probably avoid like foods high in saturated fat and cholesterol. A small amount of these things may not harm us, but it also doesn't help. Being healthy is what God wants us to be, so that we can live fully with Him in us and us in Him! Paul writes to the Corinthian Church, "Do you not know that your body is a temple of the Holy Spirit, who is in you, whom you have received from God? You are not your own; you were bought at a price. Therefore honor God with your body" (1 Corinthians 6:19). Let's live healthily devoted to God!

For the low-sodium lifestyle, here is a list of foods to generally avoid. And, it may seem hard if you learn that you have a new food-aversion or allergy, but after a while, it's really not that bad. You learn what you can and can't have, and there is still food for you. Consider, too, that God gives us diets to learn the spiritual discipline of waiting for Him, and staying away from evil. God says, "I will give them an undivided heart and put a new spirit in them; I will remove from them their heart of stone and give them a heart of flesh" (Ezekiel 11:19). Let's receive His new heart, by letting go of the old. Also, I'll let you know that when I first learned I had hypertension, I was very upset and worried. Jesus teaches us to not worry though, because He has it all planned out (Matthew 6:25-34). Plus, now that I have had to cook with no salt at home, I've learned more about cooking, and by the LORD's grace and provision, this cookbook can help others! There is a great verse in Ecclesiastes 7:14 that summarizes God's hidden blessings and how He is always there for us. It reads, "When times are good, be happy; but when times are bad, consider: God has made the one as well as the other. Therefore, a man cannot discover anything about his future."

1. You'll probably stay away from all packaged meals. Buying frozen foods is very quick, but it will quickly raise your blood pressure as well! (See 'Jay's Spicy Enchiladas,' pg. 116.)

2. Avoid store bought dips, salsas and spreads. These are very fun to make at home, and will probably give you a lot more bang for your buck. Additionally, you wont get any side preservatives. You'll just have the fresh ingredients, and learn how to custom make them for yourself and others! (See 'Humus,' pg. 33; 'Bruschetta al Pomodorro,' pg. 35; and 'Guacamole,' pg. 121 to start.)

3. All canned soups, or soups at restaurants, are out! Making soups at home is a blast though, and provides you with food for days. As a bonus, the active time of cooking is pretty minimal, so the pot is doing the work for you (really God is)! (See any of the soups from pgs. 54-65.)

4. Some canned foods have no sodium, but when they say 'low-sodium,' still look at the label. The amount is actually often very high. Otherwise, buy your own vegetables, beans, and tomatoes fresh and/ or in bulk. ((1) For vegetables, see 'BBQ-ed Vegetables,' pg. 29, 'Broccolini e Asparagi,' pg. 36, and all the salads (pgs. 38-53) to start; (2) for beans, peas and date preparation, see 'Sabrina's Quinoa Salad,' pg. 45, 'Couscous with Shrimp,' pg. 52, any of the soups (pgs. 54-65), and 'Orzo Pasta,' pg. 77; (3) and for tomato sauces, see 'Spaghetti,' pg. 71, 'Jambalaya Pasta,' pg. 74, 'Shrimp Pizza,' pg. 90, 'Bouillabaisse,' pg. 93, and 'Chicken Pizza!,' pg. 114!)

5. Remember, Jesus made you the way you are for a reason. God says, "'For I know the plans I have for you,' declares the LORD, 'plans to prosper you and not to harm you, plans to give you hope and a future'" (Jeremiah 29:11). And one of the things that He has given us to prosper is shrimp! When buying shrimp, make sure that they are wild caught and fresh! They taste so great and are so healthy for you. Praise the LORD! (See 'Salade aux Crevettes et Herbes,' pg. 48; 'Pasta ai Gamberetti,' pg. 86; and 'Shrimp and Clams,' pg. 94 to start.) Hallelujah!

6. Avoid most breads and dairy products (my only salt exception). Look for a 'no-sodium bread' or make it at home. Here is a great recipe for a no-knead ciabatta. Make it weekly without salt!

   No-Knead Ciabatta - Bread You Can Believe In. Monday, 9 Jan. 2009. Food Wishes: Video Recipes. google. Web. 26 Nov. 2011. <http://foodwishes.blogspot.com/2009/01/no-knead-ciabatta-bread-you-can-believe.html>.

7. Mostly everything at a restaurant, try to order without salt or butter. The waiters are usually very nice! Like, try getting French fries without salt. It's great! And potatoes have lots of K^+. God Bless your new gift that God has given you to be creative and learn more about Him!

Foods High in Potassium

Here is a list of foods that are naturally high in potassium in mg per serving size.[190] By eating some of these foods every day, you can help to lower your blood pressure and be more aware to move in the Holy Spirit's guidance. Paul writes to the Romans that, "In the same way, the Spirit helps us in our weakness. We do not know what we ought to pray for, but the Spirit himself intercedes for us with groans that words cannot express" (Romans 8:26). God is always there waiting for us to listen to Him. When we do, He tells us amazing things, and leads us to help others (consider Luke 5:4, and the great catch of fish that was a result of Simon's obedience to Christ).

Fruits

1 medium avocado	900
1 papaya	781
1 cup prune juice	707
1 small banana	467
1 diced honeydew melon	461
1/3 cup raisins	363
1 medium mango	323
1 cup fresh strawberries	276
1 medium kiwi	252
1 small orange	237
1 medium pear	208
1 medium peach	193
1 small apple	159

Vegetables and Legumes

1 medium potato (*Baker*), with skin	844
1 cup pinto beans	800
1 cup lentils	730
1 cup dried peas	710
1 cup cooked pumpkin	564
1 cup cooked mushrooms	554
1 baked sweet potato, with skin	508
1 cup fresh Brussels sprouts	494
1 cup fresh green beans	374
1 cup fresh carrots	354
1 cup cooked zucchini or squash	346
1 cup fresh or cooked asparagus	288
1 cup fresh broccoli	286

Meat and Proteins

7 oz baked or broiled salmon	744	12 oz yogurt	464
1 cup soy milk	690	1 cup 2% cow milk	377
7 oz roasted turkey, dark meat	604	1/4 cup sunflower seeds	241
1 Tbsp molasses	498	3 oz cooked lean beef	224

Thank and Praise the LORD that this book is here! For it is only by His mercy and love that anything is possible. Thank Him for working through my family and supporting me daily. Also, thanks to God for working in those who were led by His kindness to give generous support (Thomas Walters, Tim Assad, Jordan Johnson, and Nick Woods)! May God continue to bless them and you!

Recipes:

Bread of Life in SB for reminding of His Name (25)

Ben Ingalls for *plating* (30), the 'Creative Salad' (41) and many adventures

Sabrina Walters and family for 'Sabrina's Quinoa Salad' (45) and an always warm and welcoming home

Barbara Setniker for many years of teaching in Christ, the evening of the 'Salmon Salad' (47), many pies and 'Rhubarbara Pie' (124)

Everyone in Ensenada, Mexico (62 and 107)

Tim at *Elephants Delicatessen* for the 'Orzo Pasta' (77) and Kristin at Elephants, for graciously accepting to pose in 'An Introduction to Pasta and Carbs' (12); see also acknowledgments (3)

Jordan for many years of friendship, and yogurt-marinated kebabs (111)

Everyone at the pizza gatherings (90)

Louie Olivares for guidance (93)

The Liggetts for their amazing gift of the beach house and their love (93, 94)

Josh Tengan for a great day with 'Kale Steak' ('Jesus Loves') (101)

Jay for friendship and 'Jay's Spicy Enchiladas' (116)

Sue landgren for her delicious and nutritious 'Sue's Chocolate Oatmeal Cake*' (123)

Jesus for His Word (132) and all of our friends

Special Thanks:

Door of Hope. Thank you God for speaking through Josh White and Tim Mackie, and thank you Josh, Tim and Church family for listening.

Door of Hope
Hinson Annex
1315 SE 20th Ave. Portland, OR 97214
www.doorofhopepdx.org   . . . and of course ⟶

Thanks be to the

LORD

"Let everything that has
breath praise the LORD.

Praise the LORD"
(Psalm 150:6).

Amen and Amen

Truly, Jesus is real. Just this afternoon, a miracle happened. For about three years now, my dad had been suffering from a pinched nerve in his back and had almost been debilitated. His whole leg had gone numb and he couldn't even put on his shoes. Well, not anymore, thanks to the Living God who heals! Today, our family friend and sister in Christ, Carol Steel, came to visit us. She asked how my dad was doing. He told her the truth, and God prompted her and us to pray. After about 10 minutes, we asked him what was happening, and he told us God had healed his shooting pains! Thanks to the real God, my dad has never looked and felt better. He started to walk around the room and we praised Jesus as he did lunges, squats, and pretended to tie his shoe. God loves you. No matter what, He loves you and offers complete forgiveness and healing. Praise the LORD!!!